# SILENCING ORPHEUS

# SILENCING ORPHEUS

A NOVEL BY J. WARREN

QUEER MOJO
A Rebel Satori Imprint
Bar Harbor, Maine

Published in the United States of America by
REBEL SATORI PRESS
P.O. Box 363
Hulls Cove, ME 04644
www.rebelsatori.com

This is a work of fiction. Names, characters, places, and incidents are the product of the author's imagination and are used fictitiously and any resemblance to actual persons, living or dead, business establishments, events, or locales is entirely coincidental. The publisher does not have any control over and does not assume any responsibility for author or third-party websites or their content.

Book design by Sven Davisson

Library of Congress Cataloging-in-Publication Data

*This book is dedicated to Bruce and to Chris, both of whom helped me get it in to shape*

"Orpheus wished and prayed, in vain, to cross the Styx again, but the Ferryman fended him off. Still, for seven days, he sat there by the shore, neglecting himself and not taking nourishment...Three times the sun had ended the year in watery Pisces, and Orpheus abstained from the love of women, either because things ended badly for him, or because he had sworn to do so. Yet, many felt a desire to be joined with the poet, and many grieved at the rejection. Indeed, he was the first of the Thracian people to transfer his love to young boys, and enjoy their brief springtime, and early flowering into manhood."

—Ovid, *The Metamorphoses*,
1st Century, B.C. (Mary Innes, Trans).

# 1 • My Guitar

Women have always been my weakness.
My wife died a while back.
I wake up at night reaching for her.
Usually this wakes whoever else is in the bed up, too. Jacob sleeps through it, though. He's a deep sleeper. I guess maybe that's why I like him. When I wake up, he doesn't. I don't have to explain. I don't have to pretend to be okay. The first night he stayed with me, I thought about getting a mirror to test his breath. He goes that deep. I thought maybe he was dead. I didn't know.

The wind moves the curtains. The moon comes in with the streetlight, and I can see the curves of Jacob's back. His smooth skin. He should be with someone his own age, I think. Nobody would be faster to admit that than me. Still, this is what he wants. I don't hold him here.

Times like this, I want my guitar.

I've been watching the clock's little blue numbers move for over an hour, now. I want to get up, but I'm afraid that if I do, this might be the one time that I do wake Jacob up. He deserves to sleep. My fingers want the strings. I could get up, get some coffee, pull the guitar down from the attic and play. I could. It would be easy.

But I won't.

The boy burrows his head deeper into his pillow. I watch as the light moves over and through his hair. I've never asked him who hurt him—I just know someone did. Maybe it's the same for him as it is for me: better when no one asks. Could be why he stays.

I will never play again. I'm a little surprised by how much I still mean it. Even back when I swore I thought *you won't feel this way forever.* I do, though. It's scary.

I don't make it easy for him, that's certain.

No one in town does, either.

His breath is warm, and there's still pizza on it. His nose is too wide for his face, but I'm starting to think that maybe that's something to do with his age. I see it a lot. I start to think about women's noses, and stop myself. My brain wants to fight with me; it wants me to see pictures of women all the time. I refuse.

I said never again, and I meant it.

My fingers want something to do. I can tell. That little bit of tension behind the knuckle: it's the same feeling I'd always get after a marathon night on stage. It's the same feeling I'd get after playing Rheinhardt all night, or DiMeola. My fingers want my guitar, and they know they can't have it.

The air is cold. I should put on some sweats or something, maybe, but that'd just make noise. I try not to make noise, anymore. Through the open bedroom door, I can see the light come in through the front room window. This is a shitty little townhouse, but the city is nice. It's small, and no one knows me. Not really, anyway. I mean, they know that someone who looks like me drives in to town each day. They see me eating at the cafe. They know that sometimes I can be found out on the long pier that juts into the sound. Other than that, though, they don't *know* me.

No one does. I don't even think I do. I go downstairs and into the tiny kitchen.

I grab the coffee pot and start the water without looking. The countertop is cold on my hand. I forgot to turn the heat on. Jacob would never tell me if he got cold, and I don't feel much these days. I should have maybe thought about it. I don't think about much, these days.

I pour the water into the coffee maker, and flick the switch on. I turn and walk toward the front window. On the small overstuffed chair near the door, I can see something vague and gray. I get closer, and pick it up: sweatpants. I hold them for a second, then look back toward the bedroom. I didn't put these here. I know he did, though. I don't have to ask; I know. Just under them is a long sleeve t-shirt. It's the blue one with the college logo on the front. Every time he sees me in it, he says he likes it. He says it brings out my eyes. He's sweet, and I hate myself for a second.

I slide into the pants, and wiggle though the shirt. I tuck my hair back behind my ears, and scratch my stubble. The coffee maker bubbles in the darkness. I open the front door. The air coming in off the bay is cold. I walk out the door and push it nearly closed behind me. On the front porch, I sit down in one of the white plastic chairs. My fingers ache just behind the knuckle, and I say "No," out loud.

Never again.

## 2 • Dawn's Rose-olored Fingers

D awn comes over the tops of this town slow. It's like molasses that's been set on fire. I can hear it, like a song. It tunes up, like a symphony. I feel connected to it. I start to think about a song I remember from when I was little, but my mother sang it, so I stop. I don't want to think about her.

I can smell the coffee through the open front window. The cold of the morning is on me, in me. Something that has been burned and finally returns to its normal state must feel like this. It's relief, this cold. It's home.

The wind comes up slow, too. It's moving my hair, and I think about how long it's gotten. People say they like it. "Old men with long hair look rock and roll," Alyssa says. I guess. "That guy from Aerosmith totally looks better now then he did when he was young," she says, "that guy from Journey, too." Without meaning to, I start singing a song, but stop myself. Even after all this time, I still do it. My fingers ache. I stand up, and go inside.

I reach into the cupboard and pull down the last clean mug. The sink is piled with dishes whether I can see them or not. I pour the coffee into the mug, and the ache in my fingers subsides. The warmth helps. I wrap my hands around the cup and stand for a second. Upstairs, I hear the sink.

He brushes his teeth before he comes near me. I guess it's sweet. To anyone else, it would be something very special. I look up the stairs. To me it's just something that happens. He combs his hair with the little black comb he carries in his backpack. It's Monday. I'll have to drive him back to school before I go to work. It's nice, sometimes, that drive. It has the feel of doing something right, almost. Something I'm supposed to do.

I can hear his feet on the hollow floors. I wonder for the thousandth time when they're going to cave through. I know someday they will. I sip my coffee, and walk back outside. The chair has grown cold, again. The sun is already a tiny golden sliver in the East.

The door opens. I don't turn around. His thin arms wrap around me from behind, and his head nuzzles next to my cheek. His hair smells wild, like a creosote bush.

"In my dream, you were playing guitar," he says, "Were you playing guitar last night?" he asks.

"No," I say, "I don't play guitar."

"Hmm," he exhales, and stands. I don't know if he believes me or not. Part of me doesn't care. The wind is still for a moment, and I can smell him—the wild smell of boys in their short-lived spring. He sits down in the other plastic chair, his long shirt covering the tiny underwear I hope he has on, at least. He put his feet up on the chair, his knees coming up to his face. He yawns. "I have to go back to school today," he says.

"I know."

"I think there should be automatic graduation when someone turns 18," he says. "Then I wouldn't have to deal with their bullshit anymore." He reaches for a coffee mug. I keep it away from him.

He giggles.

"What?" I ask.

"Nothing," he says.

"No, what?" I ask.

"Just—I dunno: They think you're my uncle. If you were, that would make this whole thing even more wrong—," he starts to say.

"We have to get on the road," I say, standing.

I can tell his eyes are on me. I can tell he wishes I wasn't so removed. I know he wants me to be sad he's got to go back to the dorms for a few days before he can come back. Truth is, sometimes I hear the noise he makes around the house and it makes things feel less cold. Sometimes, though, it's all I can do to keep from yelling at him.

He stands up, and walks past me. I can see the outlines of his whipcord little body through the shirt, and his smooth cheeks carry the glimmer of the dawn. I can see him hesitate at the door: he wants to look back at me, but he's afraid of what he'll see.

It's the lover he wants, not the statue.

# 3 • Bookstore

The jeep rattles along the highway. Every time a car passes by, the wind comes in through the plastic windows. Jacob reaches over and flips the radio on. Some old song comes over the speakers; the singer's voice raspy. I reach out and shut the radio off. "Sorry," Jacob says, "I forgot." I should have yanked the thing out a long time ago. I never got around to it.

We pass a big blue sign that says "You are now leaving Trace. Come again!" Somehow, I doubt they really mean that.

"So, what did that guy want?" Jacob asks again. I haven't answered him the past four times he's asked. He means the guy who showed up at my door with the envelope. I didn't open it: I know what's inside.

"You're really quiet this morning," he says. I can hear the tension in his voice. He's thinking that it was a mistake to stay with me. He's wondering if he should do it again. I know he will, though. They're very predictable when they're that young. He's thinking that he did something that upset me. He'll blame himself the next few days. I don't care. If it isn't him, it'll be someone else.

"Thinking," I say. I don't want to hurt him, but I don't want to lead him on, either. This is what it is. He should get used to that if he's going to stick around.

"So?" he asks.

"What?" I ask.

"What did that guy want? What was in that envelope?"

"Papers," I say. The turn is up ahead. I click on the blinker.

"What papers?" he asks.

I move the jeep off the highway and onto the small two-lane that leads to the Prep school he's lived at 9 out of 12 months of the last few years. He'll graduate, soon. I wonder how I'll feel that day.

What I'll say when he asks to stay with me, because I know he will. They all do. The road is deserted—most of the students don't leave, and the faculty lives on campus, too. This is the part of the drive I like the most.

He sighs. "Fine, if you don't want to talk this morning, then can I turn on the radio?"

"No," I say.

"Why not?"

Without slowing down, I turn and look him dead in the eye, "because I said so." I glance back at the road. To the right, there's a small river. Near the school, the boys use it for canoeing. They learn how to do it like Olympic-style. Seeing the river reminds me of the dream, though, so I stop looking.

"They were the papers for a house down South. They want me to sign off on them so they can sell it."

"Who's they?" he asks. He can sense this is pretty rare; a thread that leads backward. He wants to keep it going.

"The people who own it," I say. The school is ahead on the right. I think the thing I like most about it is how old it looks: a huge square building with giant stone columns out front and enormous sprawling grounds. It looks like a prep school. He looks exactly like it—like he belongs there.

"Are you going to sign them?" he asks.

"I don't know," I say as I turn toward the gate. The security guard comes over to my window. He makes as if he's going to tap on the glass, but sees that it's only plastic. I unbutton it, and let it fall away some.

"Morning," he says, "signing back in?" he asks.

I nod. He looks past me at Jacob, then back at me. I can tell he's looking for a resemblance. There isn't one. I'm not from this country, let alone this section of it. He looks down at his clipboard. Jacob shivers because the air outside is so cold.

"Name, son?" he asks.

"Jacob Conner."

The guard looks over the paper a bit more, then scribbles something. "Okay. Have a good one," he says, cheer in his voice. His face doesn't show any of it, though. I know he doesn't mean me. The gate squeals open, and I button the window back in place. I inch the jeep forward along the curving drive. Up ahead are the large steps leading into the main building. I pull up to them, and slide the stick to neutral. The jeep hums like bees. He looks over at me. I can tell he wants a kiss, but I can't. I won't.

"Call if you want," I say. He smiles and his cheeks flush. I don't know why I do that to him. To any of them. I shouldn't.

"Okay. Bye," he says. I can hear the pause. He wants to say more, and for me to say more. I can't give it, though. I've already given too much.

The jeep gets cold as he gets out. The door closes with a squeal and a thud. I watch until he opens the huge front door of the main house and then closes it from inside. I put the jeep in first and take the circle back to the gate. I stop at the guard shack. He looks at me for a second, and I can see he wants to say something. He can't, though. Not his job. He nods, and the gate opens slow. I inch the jeep forward until it's clear, then give it some gas.

The town looks dull this morning. It looks old. The past few months, every time I make the drive into town, I wonder why I chose this one. I still don't know. It seemed shabby enough that people wouldn't ask any questions. That was alright with me. It's just a place to wait, anyway.

The whole town only has four four-way stops. It's that small. The whole East end of the town slopes down to the pier. No matter where you're at, you can see the Sound. I think I like that, too.

I got a job in a bookstore. I spend most of my time reading the books I'm supposed to be re-shelving from the return counter. Words aren't like music: I can still read things without crying. Poetry is awful anymore, anyway. Anyone with a computer can crank out fifty lines on something inane and get it published. All the real poets, all the men I knew—they're all long dead. These leftovers don't touch me—it's safe to read them.

It's mostly just me and some college kids. They come from the University two towns over. Things are that close together. The manager keeps promising he'll get some more help in before Christmas. I don't see that happening. He's a tall man with no hair on the top of his head, but a ponytail in the back. His name is Jason, but he makes the kids call him Mr. Spooner. He's got them with the "you're my *team*" speech. For a bunch of kids who've spent their whole lives face down in a book, that kind of faith speaks volumes, faked or real. They take on some pretty hefty work loads in order to keep his trust. He comes in sometime around two every day, and spends the next three hours back in his office looking at porn on his computer. He thinks we don't know.

Maybe the kids don't, but I do.

He spends most of his time avoiding me. Something about me makes him nervous. He doesn't ask me to call him Mr. Spooner. He knows I won't. I think that scares him. It's funny, too, because I wouldn't hurt him. I don't raise my voice in the petty little battles that people wage against each other anymore. Even if they weren't so petty, I doubt I'd do anything.

I walk in, and Candace is near the magazine stacks. She looks at me, one little strand of hair floating in front of her face. She will spend the rest of the day pushing it behind her ear. Her glasses catch the light from outside, and for a second they seem to be glowing. The corners of her mouth move a little, then she stoops back to arranging.

"Hey," I say, breezing past her. I don't have to ask where anyone else is: I know that Bobby, Mick and Alyssa are all out back smoking. I head for the back room.

"Mr. Spooner left a message, this morning. I saved it for you," Candace says. I have to stop after I hear her voice to catch it all. She speaks so softly. I nod, and continue to the back. Just inside the large door, I reach for the phone. The little message light is flashing. I pick up the phone and punch the pound key.

"First message," the machine says, then Jason's voice, "This is Mr. Spooner. Ask the new guy to go into my office and get the waste reports. Have him use those to start a running tally of—," he goes on and on for a few minutes. Bottom line: he's going to be away for a few days, but someone has asked him how many books he winds up pulling off the shelves to sell to the thrift stores around town because no one wants them at full price. He wants me to check on that. The pathetic little battles. I close my eyes, and hang up the phone. Somehow, I'm still the new guy.

The back door opens. Cold wind whips in. I open my eyes, and turn. Bobby has his usual dirty white shirt and a two day old beard which he will be forced to shave by week's end by Jason. Mick is, as usual, spotless, tall, thin and Queer. I wonder if he and Bobby are having a contest to see whose sideburns are longer. Alyssa's long black hair moves as she does; swaying in a wind no one else is touched by, and her breasts are non-existent.

"Hey," Bobby says. I nod hello. They all go to the rack and take down the brown smocks Jason makes us wear. In another life, another time, I'd have railed against the idea. Now I don't care enough to even bother with any emotion. This is simply what I do to get money. It's a way to spend the day, mind numbing enough to take the ache out of the fingers.

"I think I saw you this morning on my way in," Mick says. His lisp is small, but there. He has a high voice, and moves his hands from the wrists while he talks. Until I met him, I didn't think anyone was actually like that. He ties the smock on in front, then moves it around to the back. "You drive a jeep, right?" he asks.

I slide the smock over my head, tying the knot in back without looking. "Yes," I say.

"I thought so. Was there someone else in the jeep with you?" he asks. He takes his glasses out of his pocket and puts them on. Immediately he goes from being some artsy University of New York type to a kid too young for his ambition.

"My nephew," I say. By now, the cover story is so old I don't have to think about it at all. It comes out whether I think about it or not.

"Oh," he says, and walks out the door. I catch Alyssa eyeing me as she passes by. Bobby stops just in front of me.

"You should get here earlier, smoke a little with us. It makes the day go by so much easier," he says.

"No," I say. He waits. I think he's expecting me to thank him for the invitation. I don't. I walk past him to the door marked "Office." The key sticks in the lock and won't turn. I rattle the handle a bit.

"You have to pull it back a bit," Alyssa says. She's come up behind me.

"What?" I ask

"The key," she says, stepping forward. She takes the key from me, and slides between me and the door. Her hair smells like wild jasmine. "You have to pull the key back some, so it'll catch the pins. The lock is really old," she says. As if on cue, the door pops open.

"Thanks," I say. She turns to hand the key to me without backing up. Her breasts run across my chest. She's pressing them into me, and pretending not to. She looks into my eyes. Her body is warm, and tight against me.

"You're welcome," she says, without moving. I take the key, and move around her. I said never again, and I meant it. She stands in the doorway for a second, not looking back. I flip the light on in the office, and turn my back on the doorway.

# 4 • The Boss' Business

The desk is cluttered with folders. Jason is nothing if not organized. Still, the desk is cluttered with folders. On the wall is a huge bookshelf. On it, Jason keeps most of what he considers a rare book collection. Back when I still traveled, I saw books that were thousands of years old. Compared to that, a first edition *Mrs. Dalloway* is a little hard to get excited over.

The computer is on. I've never gotten comfortable with the things. Something strikes me as odd, though: why would a guy going away for a while leave his computer on?

I start moving some of the folders around. When I do, I bump the mouse. The machine starts to whir and click. I'm still moving through folders when the screen comes back to life. When it does, I stop for a second.

There, on the screen, is a picture of a naked boy. He's got a snake curling around him, and there are a group of men sitting against a wall, watching. Next to the boy, a man sits with some sort of musical instrument. It's a charm-show. I've seen them before. Everyone but the boy is dressed in the style of Persia.

I remember the hot streets, and the constant smell of something burning. The crying of the street vendors was continuous—it got so I had to concentrate to even hear them. Most of the rest of the boys were like that, too. I'd been to sea a while, but most of the boys they grouped me with were fresh off the boat. They all had those pale, big-eyed faces that you see in every war film. In fact, that's the only thing movies about war have ever gotten right, as far as I can tell you: how kids look before they ever get shot at.

The first time we came across one of those charm shows, all the boys stopped. They wanted to watch, but you could see that something in them was horrified. They'd all come from a country where to be naked meant sin. The idea of a boy standing in the street with no clothes on was horrific. They made various symbols of holy warding across themselves. I thought it was a beautiful thing; nature like that; the charming of the snake. It's a simple trick, really: children give off lots of warmth—give a snake lots of warmth on its belly, and a soft tune to listen to, and it calms down so much you can do whatever you like to it.

Still, it seemed a bit odd to find a picture like that here, back in that country where to be nude means such horrible things. Just off to my left, though, I saw the folder that Jason must've been talking about. I picked it up, and walked to the door. I looked back at the screen, but just then noticed that the screen was turned so someone standing at the door couldn't see what was on it. Something about that seemed important to me. I shut off the lights, and pulled the door closed.

"What was it that Mr. Spooner wanted?" Candace asked. She had a stack of books in her hand that seemed really heavy. I took three off the top, and set my folder on them. Her breathing returned to normal.

"I need to log some of the waste books," I said.

She nodded as if she'd expected it, and I followed her to a shelf. She set the books on top, and started to squeeze them in with each other. The section was marked "The World at War." I picked up one of the books. On the cover was a huge field of blue-green ocean with a tiny little bit of metal sticking up above it. The title of the books was *Under the Waves.*

"Submarines," she said. I looked up as she pushed her glasses back up on her nose. "U-boats. My grampa was a submariner," she said, pronouncing it right.

"Which one?" I asked.

"I don't remember the name. He doesn't talk about it much," she said.

I don't, either, I thought.

"You never check out any of the books," she said, flipping to the section in the book with photographs. The boys were all in black and white, but I could see their eyes: I could tell which ones had been shot at.

"What?" I asked

"The books. Mr. Spooner wants us to be current on what's in the store, so we can check out books, only you never do," she said, her eyes on the pictures in the book.

"I don't have a lot of time to read at home," I said.

"Oh. On account of your band?" she asked. I must've started, because she immediately said "I mean, I'm guessing—don't you have a band?" she asked.

"No," I replied, "I don't play."

"Oh," she said, "I just—you just looked like someone who played music."

"What makes you say that?" I asked.

"I thought—well, I dunno, I just thought that I'd heard Alyssa say she'd heard one of your albums or something," Candace said. I try not to rattle Candace; I can tell someone's hurt her badly in the past.

Still, I thought, this can't go any further. "I don't play music," I said, "music is a waste of time." The lie hurts, but better this way. Better this way.

"Okay," she says, moving away, "Sorry."

I shrug and finish helping her put the books on the shelf.

At the end of the day, I'm putting away my smock. I don't like the thing. I don't like what it represents, but at this point I don't really care enough to say "hate." The back door opens, and Mick starts to walk out. As usual, he doesn't say anything to anyone. They all know they're going to meet up to smoke and talk about whatever the hell college kids talk about later. Bobby makes some stupid little salute with a dumb grin, and walks out behind Mick. For a second, I wonder if maybe they're lovers. I decide it's none of my business.

Candace squeezes past me to put her smock on the wall. She pushes the strand of hair out of her eyes, and smiles at me. "Bye," she says. I nod. She walks to the back door, and a cold breeze comes in as she opens it. "You know, it might snow tomorrow," she says. The wind coming in makes her clothes move in a certain way; for a second, I'm struck by how beautiful she is. I look down at my shoes.

"No, I didn't know that," I say.

She nods to herself, then walks out the door. I'm putting my wallet back in my pocket from the locker when Alyssa walks up behind me. I can smell her wildflowers.

No, I think. "Bye," I say without looking. It's like this every day.

"We're getting together for drinks at the Chasm tonight—you should come," she says. Her voice calls to me, asks me to turn around. I won't.

"That's okay; maybe some other time," I say, and turn for the door.

"Okay," she says, "anytime," she says, quieter. I step out into the snow.

# 5 • The Boy

D o you believe in the gods?" Jacob asks. I don't know how
to answer, so I don't. "Do you?" he asks again after a while.
"I don't know," I say, "sometimes."

He waits a bit. I can tell he wants to say something. "I knew a
guy once who called himself Zeus." I look at him. "He saved my
life." I don't say anything. He rolls over onto his side, and moves his
back against my chest. He takes my arm, and drapes it over his chest.
"A man hurt me, and Zeus saved my life. He made me go home and
face my parents. This was all a while back. Things are better now," he
said, and yawned.

I waited for him to settle down into sleep. The room smelled of
both of us, together; it's warm, human. I start to remember how the
room would smell of dark flowers after she and I were together, but
I stop myself. I must have tightened my arm; he moves closer against
me. With a sigh, he drifts off to sleep. I wish it were that easy for me.
I know what is waiting for me down there, under my eyes: the tease
of a river I can never cross.

I remember the tall man on a boat, his bony hand held out for
coin. I put mine in his palm, and his fingers begin to close. They
stop, though. The hand opens once more, and the coin drops back
onto mine. I tried to climb on as the boat moved away from shore,
but it moved too quickly.

On the other shore, she stands. She has her wedding dress on,
and her veil down. Her long hair flows in a continuous wind.

She is over there, and I am over here. That is the way of it.

I wake up. I'm covered in sweat. The boy has moved away from
me, and twined about himself at the edge of the mattress. The wind
moves the curtains. It reminds me of her dress in my dream.

My fingers ache. I move off the mattress slowly, and walk to the bathroom. I grab my knife off the dresser along the way. In the bathroom, I close the door, and flick on the light. I sit down, my arm resting on my knee. I start cutting. Never enough to do more than sting, but enough. Each stripe brings a stinging clarity to my thoughts. Some part of my mind wonders how long I've been doing this.

Three slashes on my arm run with blood. I stand up and walk to the faucet. I run water over them as I take a bandage down from the medicine cabinet. I avoid looking at my reflection. I don't want to see that.

Once the arm is bandaged, I turn off the light and open the door. I can tell Jacob is sitting up in bed. I lay back down.

"Again?" he asks.

"Yes," I say.

"How bad?" he asks.

"Not very. Go to sleep," I say.

He lays quietly, but I can tell from his breathing he won't. "One of these days, I'm going to do it, too," he says. He won't. "You're not the only one with problems."

"I never said I was."

I hear his head turn toward me on the pillow. "Would you stop me?" he asks.

"Get some sleep," I say, and turn my head away from his.

"You'd stop me," he says in a way that almost sounds like a question, "I know you would. You try to pretend you don't care about me, but you do. I know you do."

I don't answer. He puts his hand on my chest. It's warm. He starts to move it, his fingertips on my skin. "I know you do," he says in the whisper that means he wants me to touch him back.

So I do.

# 6 • Music Graceful and Powerful As the Dawn

H ow many weekends have I come to stay with you?" he asks. He's sipping coffee from a blue mug. He has his feet dangling over the side of the chair on the front porch. His knees and his eyes are almost level. He's in my bathrobe, and he's so small that the seams for the shoulders are almost at his elbows. The morning light is beginning to peak over the rooftops out on the sound.

"I don't know," I say.

"I think it's a year," he says.

I don't think it is. I don't want to talk about this, though. I want him to be quiet while the sun is coming up. I remember that there was a boy, back during the war, on the boat, who would always ask me to watch the sun come up with him. I knew he wanted me to love him, to touch him, but I never would. I only wanted her. I remember how quiet the boy would get as the first rays of golden-red came up over the horizon.

Jacob looks something like that boy, in the way that all boys in the early spring of their skin look alike. I start to think about how they all resemble her at that age, but stop myself.

"A year," he says, "it's hard to believe. We should do something; celebrate, or something." He's looking at me, not the sun. He's bouncing one knee, so that his foot flops like a flag in a breeze.

"Be quiet," I say. He used to get moody when I would say that. He doesn't any more. I know he's not paying attention to the sunrise, though: he's off in his own little world, where he and I dance to old Van Morrison records in the living room, and I ask him to marry me, though none of those things will ever happen. I wonder if knowing that makes the dream all the more sweet for him.

There should be music as graceful and powerful as the dawn,

but there never will be. This is what drives poets, and composers, and musicians—the need to put notes to the dawn that will never begin to equal it. My fingers ache. The boy is staring at me.

"A year," he whispers, his eyes still half-glazed.

"Get your things together," I say, staring as the golden disc comes fully over the rooftops, and out beyond it, the sound, glittering.

He's pouting, and looking at himself in the warped reflection of the plastic window. He thinks I don't notice that he does, that he is always looking at himself. The snow on the window has evaporated, leaving fat drops behind. They move across the glass in the wind. The speedometer says 85. The stereo is silent.

My hand slips off the gearshift and hits his leg. He turns around, looking at me. His face is hopeful. He's thinking that I tapped him to say something. In his world, I wonder what it is he was waiting for me to say. I stare straight ahead.

"There is a tour thing coming up," he says, not wanting to let the moment go. "You could come and see my room, my classes."

I raise my eyebrows some, and nod my head. Out of the corner of my eyes, I see his face fall. Even if I could tell him about her, what would I say? It wouldn't matter. I pull past the Guard Shack. The fat man isn't in it. The gate is left on auto when he does that. I wonder what the headmaster would think if he knew.

I pull the jeep to a stop. Jacob looks over at me. I turn toward him. "Well, I guess I'll call you in a day or two," he says. That's been the routine for a long time now. I nod. His lips go tight against his teeth: I've disappointed him again. He opens the door, and the cold blows in. He closes it, and I put the jeep in gear.

I know he's hoping that one day I will ask him to stay. He'd settle for one day where I wait long enough for him to get up the stairs and in the door before I drive off. He's afraid that someday, I'll drop him off and he'll never see me again. That's why, when I look back at him in the rearview as I drive through the gate, I can see him standing on the top of the entrance steps, watching me go.

I should feel awful about it.

I don't, though.

As I drive past the Guard Shack, the fat old guy is back in it. He stares at me as I drive past.

# 7 • The Chasm

The Chasm is a local bar. Bands play. I don't go on those nights. The college kids go there to play pool and drink beer because Terrence, the guy who owns the place, never bothers to check ID's. The pool tables are shoddy, and the felt has been taped down some places. When a ball doesn't go in the pocket you want, and it had to cross over the tape? They call it a "Do-Over."

On Wednesdays, there's never a band. Terrence goes to church those nights, and he has to leave his daughter in charge. She's 17, with long honey-blonde hair, and I don't look at her. He doesn't want his daughter alone with "some damned banjo player," he says. Most of the bands they get in here, though, are garage rock post-punk trios, or 60s retro-rock outfits. It's a figure of speech, I guess. I go on Wednesdays because, with no band, the place is empty. All I want is a burger and a beer and some quiet.

It doesn't stop her from trying, though. People have told me she's pretty, and her voice is nice. She comes over to my end of the bar and I stare hard at my menu. I know what I want, and I bet she could tell you my order from memory. Still, I won't look at her.

Tonight, though, tonight is different. The minute I walked in, I knew it was different. I walked in and sitting at my place on the far side of the bar from the door was the Guard from Jacob's school. Out of uniform, of course, and with a Texas baseball cap on. I stopped. For a second, I thought about walking out, again, but she catches me.

"Hi," she calls from behind the bar. She says it in *that* way, you know?

I raise my hand, and walk over to one of the three booths against the wall. I sit down with my back to the Guard. She comes over and I stare a hole into the table.

"Getcha' somethin'?" she asks. She's pressing up against the lip of the table, and if I stared, I could see things. My fingers ache.

"Burger, cheese. Medium," I say, "whatever's on draft."

"You got it," she says. The tone in her voice says "and whatever else you want," only I don't.

She's gone for maybe five minutes, when I see another set of legs standing next to the table. These have gray pants on, and work boots. I look up; it's the Guard. I kinda knew this is where the whole thing was going.

"Mind if I sit?" he asks.

"I don't know you," I say.

"You do," he says, and sits across from me. I never noticed looking through the glass of that shack, but he's not very old. Something about the lighting out there and the hat makes him seem older. He and I might be the same age. He puts his hands up on the table, palm down.

"What do you want?" I ask.

"You *do* know me," he says, "that boy you're with—," he starts.

"My nephew," I interrupt.

"—the one you're always dropping off," he goes on, "I work at the school."

"Guard shack," I say, and he nods.

"So, you see, you do know me."

"Fine, I know you. Is that it?" I ask.

He laughs without making a noise, and looks around the bar. "You're an asshole," he says. I open my mouth to say something and he raises his fingers a bit off the table. "Don't get all bent out of shape, I don't mind. Thing is, I wanted to talk to you."

I don't say anything.

"Thing is, I wanted to talk to you about that boy."

The girl brings over my beer. She sets it down in front of me, and says to him "You want something else, Smitty?"

He cracks a billion dollar smile and says "Nothing you can deliver standin' up, darlin'"

She plays like she's offended, but walks away with an extra wiggle in her ass. He isn't watching her as she goes, though. He stares at me. After a moment with neither of us talking, I raise my hands up off the table and set them back down. He nods, and looks at the tabletop for a moment. I can tell whatever he's about to say, he's been thinking about it a while.

"We both know that boy ain't no more your nephew than he is mine," he says.

"Do we?" I ask.

He nods. I wait. After a bit, he says "this ain't no attempt to blackmail you nor nothin'—hell, those boys up to that school is randier than hell twenty-four-seven. You ain't the first been sniffin' around after 'em," he says.

"Is this going somewhere?" I ask.

He leans back, and squints his eyes. He leaves one hand on the table, and I notice a wedding ring. He sees me looking, and says "four years, come this may. My little girl will turn 3 in October," he says. I do the math and smirk. "You ain't got no ring, but I coulda told you weren't the marrying type the first time I saw you."

I stop myself from saying anything.

"Fries are up, Smitty," the girl says from back behind the bar.

"Thanks, darlin'" he says, without looking. Still staring at me, he says "Thing is—," he starts, then stops. He starts fidgeting with his fingers. "Thing is—," he tries again.

I close my eyes, "You want one," I say. I open my eyes just in time to see his swollen to as large as they can go. He's seconds from denying it, but the sheer panic in his eyes is enough to tell me I'm right.

"Can we—," he starts, and swallows, trying to get his eyes back to something resembling their normal size. "Can we maybe go somewhere and talk?" he asks.

I nod just as the girl comes to the table, and puts the burger in front of me.

# 8 · Smitty

Smitty's truck rattles as soon as it gets over 45 miles an hour. The radio cuts out so much that after a while, I shut it off. He wanted it on, so I made him promise only talk radio. He found a Braves game on repeat. I was okay with that.

We finally pull to a stop somewhere near the sound. You can always tell; something in the air. The sounds of the city echo differently. He gets out, and the whole truck rocks to that side, then bounces up some. I didn't realize he was that heavy. I get out.

He goes around the front of the truck. He's shut the lights off, so it's pitch dark. He brought a bottle of booze. He uncorks it, and takes a long pull. He offers it over to me. I take it, wipe the lip off, and swig. Unrefined moonshine hits me like bricks. I swallow it down, and try not to remember a drink from Greece with a similar taste. I hand the bottle back to him, and he swigs without wiping.

In another life, I would have said something about being sorry if I offended him by wiping. I'm past that now.

"Thing is—," he starts as if the other conversation was still going on. "Thing is I love my wife. My little girl, too. I would do damn near anything for them. But this thing—you know this thing gets into your mind and you—well ya' can't half hardly see straight, sometimes."

I stare at him for a minute. I chose this, but I can tell; he didn't. He doesn't want it, but it's come too far.

"Damn near everyday one of 'em comes over to the shack and needs something—whiskey sneaked in or whatever. I try to do for 'em; they don't mean no harm by it. I just—I watch 'em, ya' know?"

"Yeah," I say, and nod.

"Anyhow, they're just so damn—shit, I don't even know what the word is. I know when it's men, yer suppose to use 'handsome,' but—but they ain't handsome," he says. I look up at the moon, and somewhere there's a splash. "I just—I was thinkin' that you got your boy and—well, I guess I was wonderin' how it goes, if you catch my meanin'"

"How it goes?" I ask.

"Hell, I don't know what to call it. With women, you go courtin'—I don't know what you call it when a boy—," he says.

"Oh," I say, and cut him off. I don't know, either. I never thought about it like that. "You mean you want to know if there are others like Jacob."

"Yeah. That's what I want to know," he says, smiles, and takes a pull on the bottle. He offers it to me again. I take it and wipe the lip again. This time it goes down smoother.

I hand it back to him. He swigs again. I can't see his eyes, but I think that's better. I don't want to see the fear, the desperation. I can hear it in his voice already. He leans back against the hood, and sets the bottle down. It thunks on the hollow metal.

"How did you and yours meet?" he asks.

"It wasn't like that," I say. I see a rock near my boot. I kick it.

"How was it?"

"I work at a bookstore. He came in. He needed a book for a class. The second he spoke to me, I could see that there was something he wanted, so I gave it to him. He kept coming around until one time I—I dunno—invited him to come home with me," I say.

"That easy?" Smitty asks, and laughs to himself.

"That easy," I say. He takes a hit of the whiskey. He offers, but I don't take the bottle.

"When I was a young buck like you, it was easy. I'd think about it, but then I had a beautiful wife to go home to, y'know? We'd go at each other for a bit, and it'd go away. Now I'm older, though, and she's off most times—and now it don't go away. Them damn boys always runnin' around in their uniforms and such—," he trailed off. "When did it happen the first time for you?" he asks.

"What, with Jacob?" I ask.

"Nah, just—just in general," he says.

It's been so long. I start to think about her hair, and I stop myself. "I dunno. A while. A long time," I say. I take the bottle off the hood and swig, and hold it out for him. He takes a swig and puts it back on the hood.

"He special to ya'?" Smitty asks. Even in the dim moonlight, I can see him looking directly at me.

"Sometimes," I say. Sometimes.

The shipyard. I'm thinking about Argo. How she spoke to us. Jacob likes to watch science fiction movies, and in them the ship always talks like a woman. There's a reason for that, and I wonder if he knows it. Still, though; all those computers sound dead, hollow. She never did. When she spoke, current ran through us. Voice lightning.

Hence, Argo. Not "*the* Argo." Not a thing. Not a dead spot. A man came to the store a year or so back. Did a talk on a translation of a poem. I knew the poem as well as I had known the poet; young, brash as they all are. I remember that he had the softest skin on his ankles. I liked the way they felt against my cheeks. The way his voice broke when I was inside him. He left, though, as they all do. Married a woman, turned into a warhawk conservative, and set about trying to convince the world he'd never spent long nights naked against me. Listening to me tell the story of that first journey. I made sure he understood, though, before he wrote the poem: it wasn't just a boat, it was a living thing.

Anyway, the man was wrong in everything he'd done to the poem. Part of his book was about ships. He said that there were lots of ships that had captured "our imagination." Ours, he said. As if I was part of that. "Mayflower. Pinta, Niña, Santa Maria," he says. I see some connection, but then he goes on, "Minnow, Enterprise." I recognize them: fictional ships. His list goes on and on, filled with them. Things that never existed. Just hollow containers; vessels. Empty voices. "Notice how we don't get a name for the ships that either Odysseus or Aneas use after the Trojan war." He's right about that, but that's because neither of them would ever let anything other than their egos be more important than their own names. Besides, those were just boats. Not living things. Then he read from his translation: every time he said "the Argo," I dug my fingers into the box I was supposed to be unloading.

Tugboats push a ship out into the channel. I've been watching the last few months. Every morning. At some point that ship will be filled with sailors, men of different ages, different skill levels. An old man, a strong man full of anger, a young musician trying to make a name for himself, etc.

No matter how the story differs, it always comes back to this.

Once, though, I think I saw what the scholar meant. Just after I met Jacob. The boy was of a similar age; that shy timidness that comes over them as their first beard begins to suggest itself along their upper lip, the back of the jaw. The new body that sprouted overnight to usurp the old one; it leaves them terrified. Of all the things that blind man got wrong, he was right about that: they are never as beautiful as that very moment.

# 9 • Horizons

A new book came out where one of the stars promised to tell all about what had happened while he was on the show. A peculiar thing, to have actors break the illusion in this way. I don't think I've gotten used to that, yet. So, I was putting out copies of the book.

The boy picked up one of the other books about that same show. The one with the young captain on a five year mission and his crew of young gods. One even had pointed ears. Jacob just showed his own copy of it to me a few nights before. I know where it's stolen from, but I didn't say anything. There was no charm in it for me, though. I was there. When the boy picked it up, I saw the picture of their ship on the front cover. Then I notice how he's staring at it. I recognize that look. That cast of the eye.

Boys go wrong with no horizons. They grow wrong. Say what you will about what is and isn't a boy, but they go wrong if there is no horizon. I see it in this one's eyes as surely as if the little painting on the front cover were sitting before him, aching and straining to leap at the stars.

Because a boat is just a boat; an empty thing, a vessel.

But when the bone-deep yearning finds a hope, that hope becomes a living thing, as sure as any goddess-touched wood could ever make it. It grows a heartbeat. It speaks with thunderous poetry.

I felt sorry for him in that instant, this young man. Then, he'd already be a warrior. He'd have already formed a band of friends gone off to write their own epic. Now, he's doomed to work making someone else's food, or to pump someone else's gasoline...to spend his days stacking books, the work of other poets about other people. I started to speak to him, but he turned and left before I could tell him what we shared—the ache. The yearning impatience of the living thing still moored at low tide.

Perhaps there are those who see Argo was never "the Argo." And yet, somehow, I hope for him that such a sense dies in his chest because this?

This is an age without horizons.

# 10 • Pressure

The next time Jacob comes to stay with me, I ask him about Smitty.

"The Guard?" he asks, already stripping out of his uniform.

"Yes," I say. I haven't moved, and he's down to his underwear.

"I dunno. He's old. He gets beer for us sometimes," he says, and reaches to pull his underwear down. I grab his hand and stop him. He looks up at me.

"Has he ever said anything to you about me?" I ask.

"No," he says.

"You're sure?" I ask.

"Yeah. Why?" he asks.

"No reason," I say, and let his hand go.

"What's that?" I ask, motioning toward the book he's reading.

"Wyatt," he says.

"Petrarch," I say.

He looks up at me, his eyes go all wide "Yeah," he says.

"Which one?" I ask

"It's sonnet number 17; something about moth to a flame," he says.

I nod. "Did your teacher talk about the mistranslation?" I ask. We don't normally talk this much. I see him blink. He's thinking of a way to keep talking so that I'll keep talking.

"No; what is it?" he asks. I think the teacher probably did talk about it. Or didn't; you can't tell with teachers these days.

I walk over near him and look over his shoulder, "Wyatt couldn't speak Italian very well. He translated by sound," I say. I point to the work 'loke.' "That word," I say, "in Italian is luca," and I make sure to overpronounce it for him, like you do with kids. He nods. "which doesn't mean 'look,' it means 'light.' Can you see the difference?" I ask.

"For to withstand her light I am not able—," he says.

"No; not just what does it sound like; can you see the difference?"

He thinks for a minute; I can see he doesn't want to say the wrong thing. I wait for a minute, and think back to learning the lyre. I remember someone standing over me, waiting. I remember the urgent gut tension of not wanting to say the wrong thing. "Say the whole thing," I say.

"I can't read Italian," he says.

"Say it like you'd say it," I tell him.

He waits another minute, then says "There are some birds that have eyes designed to withstand the light," he starts, and looks up at me to check. I nod. He goes on, "and some that the light hurts, so they don't come out except at night. Others rejoice to see such a bright fire and they go to play in it, but it winds up different than they'd planned. I'm that sort, because I'm not able to withstand her light, and I can't hide in darkness because the memory of her chases me out, so my eyes, all swollen with tears—," he says, and stops. "Tears from crying?" he asks.

"And from the shock of so much light," I say.

"It is my destiny to see her, and yet I know I'm running to the fire," he finishes.

I turn around before he can look up at me.

"Was that good?" he asks.

I walk up the stairs. After a few minutes, he follows.

For a while after, we lay quiet together.

"I didn't know you knew poetry," he says. His voice is all quiet, his words round on the edges.

I don't say anything for a long time.

"Smitty wants a boy," I say.

"What?" Jacob asks. I can tell he was off in his own world again.

"You heard me."

"Why doesn't he just go get one?" Jacob asks.

"It's not that simple. He's—he's not like me," I whisper.

"I'll say," Jacob says, and his hand snakes over my hips.

"Stop," I say, and the hand creeps away. "It's *in* him."

Jacob lays quiet for a bit. I can hear him breathing. My heart is steady, but still feels slow. He turns on his side, and his hand creeps over my arm to my chest. "You want me to see if anyone likes him?"

"Yes," I say, looking at the ceiling.

"Technically, you know that you're asking me to do something very very bad," he says. In his voice is mischief, but also worry.

"Will you do it?" I ask.

Silence for a time, then "Why do you care?" he asks.

"I don't know," I say, and I don't.

"What do I get out of it?" he asks.

"What do you want?"

"I want to stay here with you more," he fires back almost instantly, "and I want you to be nicer to me."

I wait for a moment. I can feel the tension in his hand, all the way up his arm, in his shoulders.

"Fine," I say.

We lay quiet like that for a long time. I start to drift off when he moves his hand on my chest. "Some boys at school were teasing me," he says, "making fun of how skinny I am and how I walk."

I listen. I can tell in the way he said that he's working toward something.

"They say I look like a girl," he says.

I wait.

He moves his hand again, puts it right over my heart. He is quiet for a long time.

"Do you think I look like a girl?"

"Yes," I say, and put my hand over his.

# 11 • Pain and Madness

They are always crying "What are we teaching the young?!" in this country. Every newspaper rings with that cry. I know what I'd teach them. I'd say "Run!" I would tell them that their fathers wanted them dead seconds after knowing they existed. I would tell them that this never ended. I would tell them that wars are created to do the deeds for which their fathers lacked the courage. They send boys to die on the points of spears because they cannot kill them.

The old wish the young dead with every failing breath. Men wish for their sons to be sliced in two. Women wish their daughters to submit to the same rules they gave up fighting long ago; if they refuse, then they are to be killed in the square before the eyes of the world.

And all of this to say "it was not my fault."

In my dream, I'm standing on the edge of the river, watching as the bubbles still rise to surface. I want to wake up. I keep telling myself to wake up. If someone were to come along and see me, they would think *madman*, because I'm screaming "Wake up wake up wake up" to myself, and staring at the water.

Somewhere below is my Dodge, and in it, my wife.

The image that keeps playing in my head over and over again is of that stupid gas pedal I installed three weeks ago, the one with the coiled snake on it. I bought it as a gag, and I never got a chance to show her. My mind wants to see her in full wedding dress, and over and over again I see her white shoe coming down on that snake. She never could drive all that well. Not in a regular car, and certainly not that huge monster I'd unearthed.

My mind keeps going back to her stomping down on that pedal, and what must've been her expression as the car torqued up.

And her hair, drifting lazy around her head in honey'd strands, like tentacles almost. Her hair drifting around her head as the car drifts further and further down.

I wake up.

"You're awake," a tiny voice says from across the room.

I'm sitting up, my chest heaving. I'm so hot that I wonder why the sheets aren't on fire. Sweat rolls off me like rain.

I look for the person on the other end of that voice. Jacob is across the room, huddled with his knees to his chin against the far wall. I fling the covers off of me and walk out of the room. I think about grabbing the knife, but I'm not calm enough for that. This will take something more direct. Something more horrible. I go down the stairs.

In the drawer near the coffeemaker, I find the hammer. I take it out and put my hand on the counter. I raise the hammer up over my head, spreading my fingers out further apart.

"Don't!" Jacob yells, and rushes from the stairs to my side. His hand is on my wrist. We strain against each other a moment. I shove him off me. Somewhere out in the darkness, he thuds against the wall. I bring the hammer down.

The darkness goes from red to purple. The pain is immediate and powerful. It gives me something to wrap myself around on this side of the river. I can hear it calling to me, like a voice from the deep. Pain is the only way to defeat madness, I think, and it always will be. Some part of me knew that before I'd ever picked up my mother's lyre. Pain is the only way to bring men back from madness, and music is the fastest way to create pain.

Without music, it must be done with blade or hammer—with stone or brick—by whatever means necessary. It is the same with all young men full of the bluster of war. Someplace inside, they know the old hate them. This creates a madness they cannot live through. The only way to defeat it is the pain of imminent death.

Across the room, Jacob sobs onto his knees. He's old enough to register for the draft. In some far corner of my brain I think about this as I slowly wind my uncoiled self around the pain of my hand. He is old enough for the old men in suits to send him to die, but if they were to find him in my bed, they would punish him. They would kill me because I offer him comfort rather than a sword.

If men from the government came bursting in right that moment, and Jacob asked me what to do? I would say "run—run and never return to your homeland. They enjoy cannibalism too much, here."

# 12 • Poetry

The next morning, Jacob is packing his things.

I'm standing near him. Normally, I don't. Packing seems a very personal moment to me. This time, though, I know; he is frightened. Last night was something he wasn't meant to see. Up until now, it hasn't happened during the weekends. Something about Jacob's presence keeps those old monsters from the deep down near the bottom.

He pulls a book out to make room for a shirt he's left here three weeks in a row. On the cover is a picture of a man in a black suit with a cane. He's standing on rocks looking out at a vast swell of ocean.

We haven't spoken. I woke to find him already packing.

"What's that?" I asked.

He looked over at the book. "Oh, just my poetry book," he said.

I picked it up. "I was going to do some homework while I was here, but—I just never got around to it," he says, pausing.

I take the book in my hands. It's thick in the way that all textbooks such as this are. I flip some of the pages in my hand. It has been some time since I've read poetry. My mind goes to the metallic smell of passageways, tiny stairways, and the first night I spent a thousand feet below the surface of the ocean. I stop at a random page. The top of the page says "War Poems." My eyes drift over the first few lines of one. Somewhere, in the back of my mind, a music begins playing. I want to stop reading, but I can't. I look away from the book.

"What's wrong?" he asks, reaching for my arm. I slammed the book closed, and stood. The book fell. Jacob flinched.

"Nothing," I say. I walked to the door and went outside. On the porch, I leaned against the railing. It was cold and wet. My fingers began their terrible ache. The bruise is already formed, and by noon

I won't be able to use the hand at all.

Behind me, the door opens and closes. I hear him breathe. "Here," he said. When I turned, he was holding my jacket out to me. He always thinks of things like that. "I'm sorry," he said after a time.

"For what?" I asked.

"I dunno; whatever upset you."

"I'm not upset," I say. I turned to stare out across the sound.

"You are. Why do you always try to lie to me and say you're not upset when you are?" he asks. He moved over next to me. The leather of his jacket creaked. I tried to remember if I'd bought it for him.

"I don't," I say.

"You do. You're doing it right now."

"Oh," I say.

He closes his eyes and exhales. The steam drifts up past us into the dark sky. My fingers jump they ached so bad. He looks, then looks away.

"I want you to tell me things," he said.

"Why?" I ask.

"Because that's what people do when they care about each other—they tell each other things."

"Do they?" I ask.

"Yes, they do. They share things," he said without looking.

"Oh," I say. He exhales again after a while.

"Just tell me one thing, *one thing*, about who you are, and why things hurt you so bad," he says.

"Why?"

"Because I want to know. Because maybe it might help if you tell me," he says.

"It won't."

"You don't know that," he says, turning toward me.

I closed my eyes, "If I tell you," I open my eyes and looked at him, "then the burden is on your shoulders. Is that what you want? More to carry than you already have?" I asked.

He blinked.

"Isn't it just possible that me not telling you could be a gift?" I ask. He doesn't say anything for a moment. I can tell he's actually thinking about it. I shrug into the jacket. "If I were to tell you everything, Jacob, would you still want to be around me?" I ask. He doesn't answer. "Be honest, isn't half the thrill of this whole thing you not knowing anything about me?" I ask, and he shrinks a bit. He didn't think I knew that. "Some part of you loves that I am a blank canvas; that you can paint anything on me that you wish. I don't mind that—I don't interfere with that, do I?" I ask.

He's shaking a bit. He doesn't know if he should answer or stay quiet: this is the most I've spoken to him since we met. I can tell that he wants to stay quiet, hoping I will say more. I turn to him. His eyes are such clear blue that they shock me every time I see them. I put my hand on his shoulder. The bruise looks ugly and horrible next to his soft skin and pink lips. Just as Smitty said, it's not handsome; it is another word that means something more terrible and bone-chilling.

"I don't mind that you have an entirely different world for us. Just remember that if I gave you any of what you want right now, it would destroy that world forever," I say, and turn to face the dawn once more.

# 13 • That Music

Somewhere there is a music playing, and I want to be there. I want it. People who have television and radios in their cars don't get it.

Imagine depriving yourself of music because you can't stand the beauty of it anymore. Nevermind. Chances are unless you've done it, you can't understand what I mean. I'll tell you my fingers ache, but what does that really mean to you?

What does that really mean?

Because I can describe it all day long, and you can smile and nod because you were taught that's the polite thing to do. You won't get it, though. Try, though. Try for a second.

In my dreams, Jacob is standing in front of me, and I am telling him all of this. And his eyes are wide, because he wants to. He knows this is his only chance. He also knows it is hopeless. There might as well be a giant wall between us. The wall is made of glass, though—he can see me. Somehow, I think that's more cruel than not seeing me at all.

Somewhere there is a music playing; a woman behind a piano with red hair and a voice that breaks ships against rocks. I crave it in the bones of my chest, like dry tongues crave salt—finish the job, they cry, and so do I. Finish the job. Snap them like cold.

He wants to understand; his face says so.

Just before I wake up, though, I wonder if *I* want him to.

# 14 • Talk To the Boss

Jason comes to work that morning and doesn't say hello to anyone. All we hear is the door close. It's strange how you can hear that sound all the way in the front of the shop. It doesn't matter what you're doing—when the boss's door closes, we all know. It's a strange sound—almost no way to describe it. Something like God casting his favorite angel out.

I imagine that the impact must've sounded like that.

The girl I'm helping is this coltish little English major who comes in all the time. Long legs, long arms, stringy hair. She likes Neruda.

I used to know Neruda. I used to know whole books of poems by heart.

Not anymore.

Something in my eyes must've jumped when she spoke the first line, though. She saw something I couldn't control for a moment. One split second of light, and then the memory. That was a bad day. Now, every time the girl comes in, she wants to talk about Neruda with me. When that door slams, I walk away from her. I don't say it out loud, but it's a relief.

"What's going on with Mr. Spooner?" Candace asks. She was standing one aisle over the whole time. I wonder if she heard everything the poetry girl said to me.

"I don't know," I say, walking past her. I leave them both standing near each other.

The back door is still open a bit. I close it, and the click echoes. When I turn around, Mick is next to me. "Jason upset?" he asks.

I smile at the small mutiny, "Yeah."

He nods. We're both staring at the door. "You think he's on coke?" Mick asks. I turn to him. "I mean," he says, his eyes getting wide, "he's so moody."

"I don't know," I say. He nods to himself and walks away.

At that exact second, the door opens. Jason is standing there, staring at me. The bags under his eyes could hold luggage. His eyes are glazed over. For a second, I wonder if he's even seeing me.

"Come in," he says. He motions quick with his hand.

I walk to his door. He sits at his desk.

"Close the door," he says. I do. The white noise in the room gets heavy, and muffled. "Sit down," he says. I walk to one of the chairs and sit. "You been here how long?" he asks.

"I don't remember."

"I can't put my finger on it, but I trust you. I trust you more than I trust any of *them*," he says, gesturing toward the door with his chin.

"What's wrong with them?" I ask.

"Nothing, nothing at all, if you're another dumb-fuck college kid, like them. If you're another drugged-out, going-nowhere, twenty-something cliché. But guys like you and me, we're going somewhere, doing something." I decide that Mick is right; this guy *is* on something. "Guys like you and me, we got priorities. We can't sit around and let big opportunities pass us by, can we?"

I don't know what to tell him, so I don't say anything.

"No, we can't," he answers for me, and I relax. "You know where I went? Go ahead, ask me where I've been," he says. He's grinning. He laughs one little under-his-breath, laugh; that same laugh people do on airplanes when they want you to ask what's so funny.

"Are you on something?" I ask.

He waits a second, "What does that have to do with anything?"

"I don't know that we should be talking like this if you're on—," I start.

He interrupts, "I was in New York. Ask me why."

I look over at the door, then back at him. Why not. "Why were you in New York?" I ask.

He looks around for a second to see if we're alone. I almost want to look, myself. I don't, though. He leans forward on the desk. Papers rustle under his elbows. "I bought a boy."

I don't say anything.

"I bought a boy. I mean, I've done my part, right? I've married, had kids: I've done my part." As he says all this, he gestures to the picture of a pretty blonde on the desk. She's got one arm around a boy about Jacob's age, and the other one around a girl just a bit older. The girl is wearing a suit jacket and a black skirt. It looks like one of those pictures they put in the photo pockets in wallets to make you think happy thoughts. They look bland and perfect. "I've done my part, and I can have what I want."

"Bought a boy?" I ask. My voice is ice cold.

"Yes," he says, closing his eyes and nodding. He looks just like some televangelist when he does. He looks like he's just delivered some massively important piece of knowledge to his brethren. "He'll be here next Tuesday; do you want to meet him?" he says. The way he says it, I can tell he means more.

"Why would I want to do that?" I ask.

His face falls a bit. "Well, it's just—I mean I overheard the kids talking about you," he says, gesturing out the door with his chin, "they said you've got a boyfriend. A *young* boyfriend."

I stand up. "You've made a mistake," I say.

"Oh," he says. Something in him changes; his shoulders, his breathing, something. "Well. Can I ask you—umm—will you keep this—you know—," he stammers.

I don't care. "I don't care," I tell him.

As I walk out the door, I wonder if it's true.

## 15 • Jacob Speaks Of the Past

About three weeks earlier, I'd woken from one of my dreams, and needed to cut. I didn't notice that Jacob wasn't beside me. I was revved up so far into the red that I wouldn't have noticed if an elephant was lying there.

When I flipped on the bathroom light, though, Jacob was sitting on the edge of the tub. He had my razor in his hand. His forearm was smeared with blood. His eyes half lidded.

"What the fuck are you doing?" I asked, snatching the razor away from him. His eyes snapped full open.

"I was—I was—," he keeps repeated.

I slam the razor down on the countertop. I'm enraged. Instead of letting it all out safely, I grab him by the throat. He tries to stop me, but his hands are so weak on top of mine. I haul him to his feet, and then out of the bathroom. I fling him onto the bed. I'm on top of him in moments, and he's struggling beneath me.

It isn't until the dim light from the bathroom shows his eyes drowned in tears that I stop. He's crying so hard he can't breathe. His face is red.

I flop over off of him onto the bed. He's shaking. Dimly, somewhere at the back of my mind, I know I need to hold him. That he deserves to be held. That I am a bad person. But for that moment, I can't do it. I can only lay there.

He calms down slowly.

"I didn't think you were going to stop," he says, his voice gravelly from the exertion. I can't say anything. "I thought that all that stuff Zeus got me out of was coming back," he says. "It just all made sense for a second: that I had gotten away for a bit, but that it was time to pay up." He goes still for a moment. He's not shaking, anymore.

Then he rolls over onto his side, and drapes himself across me.

He buries his head against my neck. "I thought it was time to pay up, finally," he says. We're like that for a long time.

"See, my dad didn't want me around when he found out. He caught me in bed with—Jesus, what was that kid's name?" he asks. His voice is muffled against my skin. I've calmed down to the point that I wonder, too. "I can't remember the kid's name, but it was this boy from down the block. My dad caught us in bed together. He kicked me out." He moves his head some, and his cheek is against my shoulder. "He was a minister, you know? He couldn't abide that sort of thing going on in his own house, he said. So I left and went to New York. The city, not the state; I already lived there." He pauses for a few moments, and I find myself listening.

He moves again, and I can tell he's staring at the ceiling. His hair is near my face, and it smells the way only a boy's hair can after sleeping. "I wasn't on the streets long before Jimmy Paris found me. I guess it's dramatic or whatever, but I felt like I was half dead. At first, I thought he was just another guy who wanted me to touch him. I'd done some of that to get money for food or whatever. He wanted more than that, though." Jacob's grip on me tightens, and for a second I wonder if he even knows it has. His voice sounds far-off. "He said that I could be warm year round, and instead of all the different men doing stuff to me, it could be just one. At first, I thought he meant him. He wasn't that bad looking, so I said 'ok.' Turns out, though, he worked for this other guy who sells boys to men. He told me that after we were already up in his hotel room. It was weird, too, because it was like he had it timed. He told me that and then the room went fuzzy. He knew exactly how long whatever he'd slipped in my coke took to kick in. Then I remember—," he starts to say, then fades. I almost think he's asleep, but he says "I remember him saying he needed to 'test out the merchandise' before he could deliver it. He did—things—to me. Hurt me."

I hadn't realized it, but my hand is over his. I'm rubbing his fingers. I wait for the panicked feeling to hit me, but it never does. Jacob says "I don't know how long we were there, but then this guy busts in and puts a gun in Paris's face. The guy takes Paris in the bathroom and shoots him. The screaming—the screaming was horrible. I guess this guy shot Paris in the stomach, and then left him to die with the lights off. Then he came in and checked on me." Jacob's spine is mostly relaxed from where it had gone ramrod straight earlier. "The guy tells me his name is Zeus, and that he's going to take me home. He did, too. He had some other boy to save, but he took the time to make me go home. When I showed back up, the old man was already broken because of some other stuff that had happened. He didn't last long. For a second there, I thought that all this time had only been borrowed. I thought maybe it was time to finish dying," Jacob says.

I can relate.

# 16 • Next Tuesday

What's wrong?" Jacob asks. His hands are on my shoulders. He's not doing any good, really, but I don't stop him.

"Nothing," I say.

"You're lying again," he says flatly.

"It's Tuesday," I say.

"What?" he asks. His fingers stop.

I stand up. I walk over to the window, and open it. As if on cue, a plane flies by over head. The sun is going down.

"This isn't about—I mean, I know I can't stay over. It's a weeknight and all. I won't stay. I just wanted to hang out a bit longer, you know?" he says, and I can hear him getting sad. "I can catch a cab," he says, "You don't have to—."

"It's not about that," I say.

"Oh," he says, quietly. He moves up behind me, and his hands are on my back. "What's it about?"

"Jason," I say.

"The guy who owns the bookstore?" he asks.

"Yes," I say.

"What about him?"

"He's done something—something because of me."

"Like what?"

I turn a bit, so I can see his face out of the corner of my eye. "He bought someone."

"*Bought* someone? What's that mean?" he asks.

I walk away from the window. "Just what I said: he bought a boy."

Quiet. Then he says "You mean like—?" he asks.

"Yeah," I say, sitting down on the bed, "that."

He mouths the word 'oh,' and comes over to sit down next to

me. The bedsprings don't squeak: he's still too thin. "Maybe it's not that bad. You said he was a decent enough guy, right?"

"I don't know," I say.

"I mean, if he's a decent enough guy, then maybe its okay. It could be worse, right?"

"That's not the point," I say. After a bit I say, "he did it because he heard rumors about me and you. He thought that if I could do it, then so could he."

"Getting away with it kind of thing, huh?" Jacob asks.

I turn to look at him. The dark red light frames his face like a rose. Sometimes he amazes me. I stop myself from thinking how much like her he is. My fingers ache. "Yeah."

"So," he says after a time, looking away, "what does that mean?"

"I don't know, yet," I say. But I can tell he knows exactly what it means: I've been here too long. People are starting to talk, and I'm going to have to move on. I think he sensed it the second he met me. "I don't know."

# 17 • The Brechert Gap

No matter how much you try to heat up a submarine, it's always cold. The cold comes in from the walls, radiates through the floors. That's under the best conditions. When you're traveling under an ice shelf, things get much worse. Every minute, you have to stop yourself from remembering that you are buried under almost a thousand feet of water which is covered over by ice hundreds of feet deep." The old man was speaking in slow, round tones, the way old people do when they know they have an audience. Mick was watching the front of the store, and Bobby had disappeared. Candace was out sick, while Alyssa and I were taking care of Thomas. Old guy. Lots of time on submarines. Every time we got a new war book in, Spooner would dig him up to come do a talk.

When you live too far away for a book tour to ever come through, this is as exciting as it gets. I'd never been in the store for one, before, though.

"You'd figure that many people crammed together, like a can of people, would generate some heat. They didn't, though. I remember thinking several times a night that I was going to wake up to frostbitten toes. I just wanted to climb in with someone else and snuggle, even though I hated them all. Well, maybe not all of them, but you get the idea. I thought that I should pick someone fat; they seem to sweat a lot. I'm guessing that means they're warmer. I don't know."

He pauses for effect. "True, this was a while back, too. I mean, they might have some sort of warmers on the things, now. A heater of some kind. They didn't back then, though."

"What is it?" Alyssa asked.

I hadn't realized I'd been grimacing and shaking my head. "Nothing," I said.

"That wasn't a 'nothing' look. What?" she asked.

I looked over at the old man, who was leaning in close to the front row of his "audience," a row of kids. I shook my head again, and looked back at her. "Nothing."

She shook her head, too. After straightening a few books on the nearby shelf, she said "You gotta' hand it to the old fart."

"Hand what?" I asked.

She looked over at him, then back at me, "He has a way to stay needed." I looked at her. Something had changed. She was almost whispering. The skin around her eyes was dark. Her hand lingered on the spine of a book. I nodded. Her eyes stayed on mine. I looked away.

"Cigarette?" she asked. She always asked.

I shook my head.

"Come on; I don't want to have to smoke by myself."

I followed as she walked out. The door squeaked some. From the back door, we could look down into the ditch beyond a small metal fence. After the rain of the last few days, a little river ran through it. The gurgling water made a noise filled the silence. She pulled the cigarette out with her fingertips, and placed it between her lips. She covered half her face with the palm of her hand, and I heard a click. When she took her hand away, she puffed smoke out the sides of her mouth.

"What was it back there?" she asked, exhaling.

"He doesn't know what he's talking about."

"What do you mean?" she asked, inhaling again.

"He's making shit up. It wasn't like that."

Her eyes opened a bit, then went dull again. She exhaled. "How do you know?"

"I served on a boat like the one he's talking about." I looked at my watch. In another hour I'd be off work. Jacob would want me to come get him.

"No," she said.

"What?" I asked.

"No, you didn't. If you did, you'd have to be as old as he is," she said.

I didn't respond. I watched a red leaf float down the stream.

"Why do you do that?" she asked.

"Do what?" I asked back.

She exhaled, and tilted her head to the side, "That. That whole 'I'm above answers' thing?"

"I don't know what you mean," I said. I put my hand on the doorknob, and turned it. She looked down at my hand, then back up at me. I waited a second, then went in. The door clicked shut behind me.

"So, when we got to the Brechert Gap, I decided to bail out. I'd had enough. The rest of the crew had, too," the old man was saying. "We decided that we would get to the surface, and make for Havana. It would be better to be a Communist someplace warm than a patriot under ice!" he said with a smile. The audience gasped. The kids were all young enough to think the word "communist" was dirty. The old man smiled.

I walked over to the group. "Time," I said. He looked up at me, and his smile faded. The kids groaned. Some of the adults standing nearby barely hid the looks of relief. They shuffled the kids along toward the door. Some of them stopped to hug the old man. He smiled at them and hugged back.

After they were all gone, the old man stood. "Bad timing," he said, "bad timing all around." He hobbled over to his cane, then attempted to stand up straight. "You look very familiar young man," he said.

"I should," I say. I hadn't moved.

He squinted. After several long moments, he nodded, then hobbled past me toward the door.

# 18 • The Unwelcome Passenger

So, you knew the guy?" Jacob asked, toweling off his hair. My eyes traced his lean body. I remembered how shy he'd been the first few times he'd stayed with me; how he'd take all of his clothes with him, and emerge fully clothed after a shower.

"Yes," I said.

"How?" he asked.

"We were lovers, once."

He stopped toweling for a moment, looking at me from beneath his eyebrows. "But you said he's old."

"He is."

He let the towel fall away from his head, and rested it over his shoulders, pulling on the corners. It made a cape over him, in the fashion I'd seen growing up. I thought for a moment how beautiful he would have been under the Tuscan sun.

"I don't understand," Jacob said.

I walked past him, "There are some people that death won't take," I said.

"What?" he whispered, following me.

"Nevermind," I said. I walked toward the front door.

"Please tell me," he said, stopping on the stairs.

"No."

"Where are you going?" he asked.

"For a walk."

"Can I come with you?" he asked.

I didn't answer. The door closed behind me.

# 19 • Death Stopped For Me

Halfway down the block, he catches up with me. He has my coat in his hands. He hands it to me without breaking stride. He whips his scarf around his neck. I think for a moment that on any other day, on any other person, the gesture would be endearing. He doesn't say anything, but falls into step beside me. He shoves his hands down into his pockets.

"You've got a past. I'm okay with that," he says. From a woman, these words would make sense. From him, they don't. I wish I knew why. As we turn back onto the street my apartment is on, he puts his hand on my arm, and stops. "Please stop," he says. I do. "Is it something I said that makes you not want me around?"

"What makes you think I don't want you around," I say after a while.

He looks down the road, and then back at me, "this."

I look at him for a time, then say, "I want you here, with me."

His smile dawns over his face slowly. I turn and walk away, again. I can hear him following. "You don't have to open up if you don't want to, but—I dunno. You don't always have to be so secretive."

We're silent the entire walk back until I walk up the steps to the front door. Without looking back at him, I say "To you, old means one thing. It means college, and then a job, and then a house. It means a lot of things that it doesn't mean to me," I say, walking in the door. I take the jacket off and throw it on the couch.

He closes the door behind us. "What does it mean for you?" he asks.

I turn toward him. He's stopped at the door. Bundled up like that, he looks lost. He looks even younger than he is. I can feel something in my chest move at the sight, but I don't let it go any further. "I already told you; for some people, death will not stop."

"Emily Dickinson," he says.

"What?" I ask.

"Emily Dickinson. It's a poem we've studied. I dunno; I thought you meant the poem or whatever," he says, looking at his feet.

"No," I say, walking upstairs, "that's not what I mean."

"You've read it?" he asks, his face lighting for a second as he looks at me.

"No," I say, "I haven't."

"I could let you see it," he says, his voice gone quiet. He looks at his feet again. I can tell he wants me to see it, to like it as much as he does.

"Poets are liars," I say, "they take the facts and twist them. Poets are worse than any newspaper reporter or nightly news anchor. Trust me. If this Dickinson woman wrote something about death, she doesn't have the slightest clue about it."

He looks hurt. I might as well just have slapped him. I continue upstairs, stripping off as I go. I can hear him coming up them as I slide between the sheets. He stands at the door for a moment, the room in complete darkness. All I can see is his outline in the moonlight coming through the window. He's still in all his clothes. He stands there for a while.

"Get in bed," I say, and he starts to strip.

# 20 • Not-yet-a-man

D o you think what we're doing is right?" he asks, not looking up from his plate.

I stop. The tension in the room jumps.

"What do you mean by 'what we're doing'?" I ask.

He carefully sets down his napkin on the table. I think he knows he's crossed a line. For a second, I wonder if he's noticed the packed suitcase under the bed. I wonder if he knows that I'm leaving, soon.

"I just meant—you know: *us*."

"What do you mean, 'is it right'?" I ask.

"Nothing," he says, still picking at his food with his fork, "forget it."

I go back to eating, but I know that it's not that simple. After a few minutes of silence, I set my fork down, and look at him. "Pay attention, because I'm only going to say this once," I say. He sets his fork down slowly, as if he's not controlling it. His eyes glue to me. "In the eyes of three-quarters of the world, you are long since an adult. It is only here, in this backward mistake of a country that they say you're not capable of making your own decisions. They're wrong about that. Where I grew up, you'd already be old enough to be a general in an army. I know this, because I *was* one. Where I grew up, it was no one else's business who a man slept with, so long as he did his duty in war, and eventually married, producing a child. It is only recently, in these self-important times, that people have forgotten who they were. So, I am a man, and you are judged not-yet-a-man, though you're close by their standards. It just so happens that I *did* my best to—," I start to say, but stop myself. My fingers hurt.

He's leaned forward, listening with his whole body. My stopping leaves him hovering between words and nothing; he desperately clings to the words.

"Your best to—?" he asks, leaving the question hanging there between us.

"Nothing. It's not important," I say, and leave the table.

The next morning, he comes down the stairs drying his hair. Again, the white towel almost shocking against his skin still red from the hot water. I watch him walk, the way his belly doesn't come out as far as his hips do, thinking about how I used to be coltish like that when I was young. Every movement is like a little symphony at that age, though they don't see it, each thing setting off an effect with every other thing. I look away.

"I've been thinking about what you said," he says to me.

"What did I say?" I ask, looking out the window at the Sound.

"About the Army," he says. He stops just behind me. I can feel his heat on my back.

"Don't," I say.

"You don't even know what I'm going to—," he starts.

"I do," I say. And I do. They all say it at some point. The need to belong to something bigger than themselves takes them all eventually. I think it's their way of dealing with me and what I am. "It would be a waste."

"Why do you say that?" he asks.

"This Army—this upstart little tin-plated Empire—it's nothing. It's a speck on the wall of the world. They swagger and fling bullets around, true, but eventually?" I say, and let the word hang. "It would be a waste. These Generals don't believe in their soldiers as anything more than convenient ways to stop enemy bullets, and they don't believe in what they're fighting for at all. They send good boys, strong boys off to slaughter like they were feeding meat into a grinder and call the boys cowards if they see the futility of it. No," I say, "don't. Do something worthwhile," I say.

"Like what?" he asks.

I want to answer him, but I find I don't have one.

# 21 • The Song

The dream is almost real. I'm lying under a huge tree. The wind whispering through its leaves makes me almost sleepy. My instrument is on my leg, and I'm strumming a tune I'm thinking of writing. I look up, and there's a lion at my feet. I want to jump up, run away, do something to save myself.

The lion is licking his paws. He doesn't even look up until he realizes I've stopped playing. Somehow, in his eyes, I can see that's why he looked over at me. He doesn't say anything, but I can tell; he needs me to play some more.

He needs it because he's hurt. He went out to hunt, and when he came back his female was dead. My song changes. Soon, I'm surrounded by animals, all of them laying near one another, listening. My song goes on and on, and I'm thinking that my fingers should be tired, but they aren't.

I wake up in the middle of the night, after the lion looks over at me, and in his eyes I saw it—recognition.

Jacob is breathing next to me. As usual, he's curled himself into a ball, and fitted himself against me. Sometimes I wonder how he does it without waking me. I can smell him sleeping. I know how silly that might sound out loud, so I never say it, but I know—people smell different when they sleep.

I reach out my arm, unaware of why. I put it around him, and press my hand, palm down, to his chest. I can feel his heartbeat. The warmth of him. He moves, digging his head further into the pillow, and I withdraw my hand.

I turn over, and go back to sleep.

## 22 • The Guard's Wife

Driving up, the guard shack is empty. I pull past the open gate to the steps and put the jeep in neutral. It hummed as the cold wind tried to rock it.

As soon as he started down the steps, I knew something had happened. His eyes were all swollen up, and he was walking slow. He never walked slow. He opened the jeep door and got in, but didn't say anything. I put it in gear and moved off.

"What happened?" I asked, a few minutes after we got on the freeway.

"I don't want to talk about it," he said.

I shrugged. He looked out the passenger side window. The snow would be falling soon.

"Brian got beat up," he said.

"Who's Brian?" I asked.

He turned his head and looked at me, "you asked me to set the guard up with someone. Brian liked him, so I introduced them about a month ago." He looked out the windshield.

"Who beat Brian up?" I asked.

"The guard guy's wife."

My stomach clenched, "Why did she do that?"

"She caught them," he said. I felt that feeling. "At least, she *says* she knew what was going on. She knew Brian, sure enough," he said. He put his hand to his forehead and leaned against the door.

"How bad?" I asked.

"Bad," he said without moving. "Hospital bad," he said after a bit.

"Is that where Smitty is today?" I asked.

"I don't know; I guess," he said. The jeep got very quiet, despite the howling wind outside. Snow started to hit the windshield.

"Why do you think she attacked this Brian kid instead of Smitty?" I asked.

He whispered, "I don't know."

"How did you find out about it?" I asked.

"Tim told me this morning," he said.

"Who's Tim?" I asked.

He turned his head to look at me, "You're really interested in all this?" he asked.

"Yeah," I said. I could see in his eyes, he thought it was because I'm interested in him. Really, though, I'm just getting more confirmation; it's that time, again.

"Tim is this boy that likes Brian. Thing is, Brian doesn't like him, 'cause Brian likes men."

"How did Tim find out?" I asked.

"I dunno; however it is people who like people find out stuff," he said with a shrug. He looked forward, "We're gonna' miss our turn," he says. *Our* turn, he says. My knuckles are tight on the steering wheel.

Jacob went silent for a bit, then asked "do you have a wife?"

I saw out of the corner of my eye that he was staring directly at me. Sometimes I wonder if he knows when I'm lying and when I'm not. "No," I said, and turned on the blinker, and pulled the car onto the off ramp.

# 23 • A Mirror

We're learning about Achilles, and the war against Troy," Jacob says. The heater is going, and the melted snow forms big drops of water on the window.

"Ilium," I say.

"What?" he asks.

"Ilium. Don't say Troy. Only the low class call it that. Homer says Illium, and you should say it, too." The blind man didn't get much right, but at least he got that part down. He looks over at me strangely. "What did they tell you about Achilles?"

"That he was a great man, and—," he says.

I shake my head, and he stops. "Achilles was no man," I say.

"I don't understand."

"Achilles wasn't a man. He was a demigod," I say. Jacob is silent, leaning in. "I don't know why men always forget to teach their children about that," I say, though I don't want to. Sometimes I feel myself unable to keep things in around this boy. "Achilles was no more a man than—," I start to say, then trail off.

"Than who?" Jacob asks.

"It doesn't matter. Achilles was a demigod. Always remember it. He can charge into battles the way he did because he has no fear of death—it cannot visit him," I say.

"But he did die," Jacob says.

I shake my head.

"He didn't?" Jacob asks.

"Don't confuse a poet's need for an ending with fact."

"But I thought you said you didn't believe in the Gods."

I look at him a moment, then say, "Believing and believing are two different things."

"I'm confused, then," Jacob says. His voice means he's humoring me.

"What else are they teaching you?"

"About Patroclus, his best friend."

"His lover," I say.

"What?" Jacob says, laughing a bit.

"His lover. Do you think that you'd go charging into battle with the greatest champion of mortal men, and then exact such a horrific revenge on him just for a 'friend?'" I ask.

Jacob is taken aback by this. He thinks. When he thinks about something, really thinks about it, he lowers his head and stares at his knees. I wonder if he realizes he's doing it.

"If Patroclus was a man—,"

"A boy," I say.

"—and Achilles was a demigod, then why were they lovers?" Jacob finally asks.

I turn the wheel, pulling into the parking lot of the apartment complex. "Vanity," I say.

"What do you mean?" he asks.

I pull the jeep into a space and shut it off. "If a man loves another man these days, what is he?" I ask. I open my door, not waiting for an answer. I know the one he'll give.

"Gay," he says.

"Which means what?"

"That he loves other men," he says, closing his door. He re-opens it, remembering to lock it this time, then closes it once more.

"It means more than that; it's an entire way of living," I say. We walk up the steps. "Then, it was different. A man was with whomever he wanted. So long as he eventually married and had children, it didn't matter." I open the front door and walk through. I hear him stop, close it, and turn the deadbolt behind me.

"I don't get it," he says. He sets his backpack down on the couch.

I stop and turn, "A man sometimes wants a real person to talk to; other times, he wants a mirror to reflect his greatness back to him. Patroclus was a boy; not really old enough for battle. Yet Achilles brought him along, anyway," I say, shaking my head. "If that boy was a mortal, could he ever accomplish as much as Achilles?"

The boy thought a moment, then said "no."

"Then why would Achilles want Patroclus close to him during a war that he clearly wasn't ready for?"

The boy thought a moment, then said "as a mirror to reflect back his achievements?" I nod. "But, then, why was the woman that was taken from him such a big deal?"

"Not for love; it was the principle of the thing. If I take something from you, it doesn't matter what it is—even if you don't want it. You'd get angry at me because I took something," I say. I sit down on the couch.

He sits down next to me. I can see him waiting for just the right length of time, then he curls himself into me, and lays his head on my chest. "So why did he get so mad when Patroclus was killed?"

"You mean, why did the mirror mean so much?"

"Yeah," he whispers, his eyes closed.

"Who am I without someone to reflect all my greatness back to me?" I ask. I push some of his hair away from his face. It smells like unpicked strawberries—wild, and a little sour. I realize this is the most we've spoken about anything in a long time. My fingers ache.

# 24 • Sammy

I'm at Chasm again about a week later. Smitty hasn't come around here in a while. The place is empty except for me, the cook and the waitress. She smiles at me every time our eyes meet. She's reading some magazine with big pictures of nearly naked women in it. I try not to look at them.

The door opens, and Jason walks in. Just behind him is a boy. The kid's hair is messed up, and his pants are practically falling off. His denim jacket is old and has patches on it from a few different bands. His eyes scan the entire place in one swoop. His socks show through his shoes. Jason is in his usual suit-and-tie combination; gray on gray with a long and very expensive looking jacket over the top. I can see from the twitch in his eyes he's on something. They walk to a booth and sit down.

When I look up, again, Jason is ordering, and the kid is looking directly at me. The waitress walks away, and Jason says something to the boy. After he does, he gets up and walks over to me. He sits down on the stool to my left.

"Hello," he says, grandly. He reaches out as if to pat my shoulder blade with his palm. I look at his hand, then back at him. He put his hand back on the counter. "How've you been?" he asks.

"Fine," I say.

"Come over and sit with us," he says. His smirk says he understands exactly what he's asking.

I look over his shoulder, then back at him. The boy was piling sugar packets into his iced tea, making a floating mountain of white crystals. "'Us'?" I ask.

"That's Darius, the—umm—the boy I was telling you about."

I nod. He stands up, and says "Little boy's room," and walks away. The boy is looking at me, again. I recognize the look; Jacob

63

had it the first day he walked into the bookstore. I stand up and walk to the booth.

I sit down across from the boy. He looks up at me, and I can tell that he's just sized me up. He's not new at this.

"Darius?" I ask. He grins too fast. "What's your name, kid?" I ask.

"Darius," he says. His voice is gravelly, but still a boy's.

"What's your name, kid?" I ask, again.

"Darius, I already told you," he says. His brows knit together.

"Last chance; what's your name, kid?" I ask.

He waits a moment, letting my vague threat sink in. "Sammy," he says, with a sigh, as though he's been wanting to tell someone for a while.

I nod; "Sammy," I repeat. He stops fidgeting and looks directly at me. His eyes don't trust.

"Who'r you?" he asks.

"I work for Jason," I say. "How long?" I ask.

"How long what?"

"How long?" I ask again.

He sits back, his eyes still centered on me. "A few weeks if it's bad; a couple months or so if it's good," he says.

I nod, "How many so far?" I ask.

"Fuck; what'r you, a cop?" he asks, looking at his hands again.

"No; but I know what you are. How many so far?"

"Third this year," he says.

"New York?" I ask.

"If I can; depends on how much I can get from him," he says. His voice almost boasts. "Do you care?" he asks.

I stand up, and walk back over to my seat. The waitress brings my food at that exact moment. Jason comes out of the restroom, and leans in close to me. "He's hot, right?" he asks.

I look at the waitress; she's staring at a large picture of a woman stretched out on a beach. I look away, and say nothing.

## 25 • Mick's question

I'm outside. On breaks, I like to go outside the store. The door opens, and Mick comes out. He's got on a tie today. He takes his cigarettes out of his pocket and taps the pack against his wrist. He shakes one out from the rest, and pulls it from the pack with his lips. He puts the pack away, and searches his chest pocket, then his back pockets for something. Finally he reaches into his jeans pocket and takes out a lighter. He holds his fingers over the cigarette and closes his eyes. He puffs twice and only then do his fingers touch the cigarette.

He looks over, as if noticing me for the first time. "Oh, shit. Hi," he says. His lisp is very soft. I nod my head at him. "Out here all alone?" he asks. I raise my eyebrows. "Not much of a talking mood, huh?" he asks, exhaling smoke. He coughs twice, holding the cigarette in one hand, and balling the other into a fist in front of his mouth. "Shit," he says after. We stand near each other, not speaking for a while.

"Can I ask you something?" he asks.

I look at him.

"Are you gay?" he asks.

"Why?" I ask in return.

"I dunno; I was just wondering."

"No," I say, "I'm not."

"Oh," he says. "I am," he tells me after two puffs of quiet.

"I know," I say.

"That's so funny, though," he says, "I could swear I've seen you checking out guys."

"Excuse me?" I ask.

"Just—you know; watching guys in the store. Looking at Bobby, or whatever," he says.

"Looking at Bobby?" I ask.

"Yeah. I mean, it's cool either way; we all stare at Bobby," he says, smiling to himself. "Don't you?" he asks, looking up at me from under his eyebrows.

"No," I say.

"So, that kid; he really *is* just your nephew?" he asks.

"Why?" I ask.

"I dunno," he says, "I've just seen him around. He has that look, y'know?"

"What look?"

"That happy look; that look guys only get when someone is taking care of them," he says.

"No," I say.

"I just thought you weren't saying anything because of how young he was. I mean, no difference to me. I was about that young when I got my first boyfriend. He was like thirty or so. You're like thirty, right?" he asks.

I don't say anything. I look at my watch. He takes another puff off his cigarette, and tosses it away. We walk through the door and back into the shop.

# 26 • An Invitation

A nnual Christmas party," Bobby says to me as I come in.
"What?" I ask, stopping.
"Christmas party coming up," he says, "free booze and a great chance to see if Candace likes you," he says, wiggling his eyebrows.

"If Candace likes—what are you talking about?" I ask, moving between shelves.

He's keeping up on the opposite side of the shelf, "Yeah! She gets drunk every year off rumballs, and then she starts to—," he stops, and looks dead ahead.

Candace is standing at the end of his row. I keep on walking, and she's just staring.

"So, are you gonna' come?" Alyssa asks. Immediately after, she puts the cigarette back in her mouth. The cold makes her smoke faster.

"To what?" I ask.

"The party. I heard Bobby talking to you about it earlier."

"Why is it so important that I come to the party?" I ask.

She looks off in the distance, squinting her eyes. She inhales, then exhales, and holds the cigarette away from her mouth, "to be social," she says.

"Why does that matter?" I ask.

"Fuck," she says, shaking her head.

"What?" I ask.

"Nothing," she says.

I let the quiet stretch between us. I know better than to think that this will be all. "*Nothing,*" she says, "it's just that—we've all gotten kind of like, close, or whatever. You don't seem to want to be, though."

I don't. "I don't," I say.

"Why not? Why don't you like us?" she asks.

"What do we have in common?" I ask.

"What do *any* of us have in common? Mick is queer, Bobby is a fifth year freshman total loser pothead, and Candace is an iceberg who reads Nietzsche. So what? Come be with us," she says.

"And Spooner?" I ask.

"What does it matter what he is or what he thinks," she says, "Did it ever occur to you that people here like you, and want to hang out with you?" she asks.

It hadn't.


I'm putting a few copies of a "new" spy thriller novel on the shelf, and I can see her wanting to talk to me. The sideways glances at me, the lingering over a shelf for more than ten minutes; it's predictable. I'm hoping I can get the last few copies in place before she—.

"Is it any good?" she asks. As if I've read it.

"I don't know," I say.

She kneels down. I try not to roll my eyes. "Fleming was a genius." She has long brown hair. I don't look at her eyes.

"Hmm," I say. I make sure not to look at her, but she moves closer.

"I wonder about all these people who have taken up his character, though. Most just do it for the money," she says. She reaches just past me and takes one of the copies off the shelf. I don't look at her arm. Or her fingers lingering over the spine of the book before taking it.

This happens a lot. People showing interest in me in the bookstore. Women, mostly. Mick calls it "cruising." I wish there was type of ring to wear to warn them off. A red hourglass. Something.

"I've seen you here for a while, and I've—," she stops herself and smiles, secretly, shaking her head a little, "I've wanted to talk to you for a long time."

I'm thinking about chord changes. About how gracefully A minor slips into G. My fingers ache. I slip the last copy from the box into the hole she just created on the shelf and stand. "I'm married," I say. I practically have to step over her to move down the aisle. I slip through the door into the back room. Without looking, I toss the box into the pile of others waiting to be broken down, crushed. I don't have to watch it land; that pile has always been there, unchanging, since long before I arrived.

# 27 • A Party

In my head, the whole way to Spooner's place, I keep hearing Jacob's voice. "You should go," he kept saying, but in that pouty way boys his age get. The one that means, secretly, *don't go.* I know it very well, by now. That's funny, because all I ever do is what I want. I never try to stop anyone from doing what they want.

Spooner's place is out near the sound. Being this close to the water makes my fingers hurt. I try not to look. For the most part, I'm successful.

I pull up into his driveway, and most of the other cars I see every day are there: Mick's sports car, Alyssa's big import sedan, and Bobby's truck with the stickers in the rear window. Up near the garage doors is Spooner's car. The lights next to the walkway to front door shine almost right on the little blue and white logo on his trunk. That's no accident.

I park the Jeep, and turn it off. I can see shadows moving around behind the lowered window shade. I can already hear the music as it rattles the window. I think about turning the jeep back on, and even reach for the keys. Before I can, though, someone looks out the shades, and the front door opens. Alyssa stands in the doorway, gesturing for me to come up. I can't leave, now.

In my own head, I think it's funny that I feel that way. I've killed men, but I can't turn the jeep back on and leave.

"Hey," Bobby says, his face lighting up as I walk in. He's talking to two girls who look barely old enough for the shirts they're almost wearing. Alyssa takes my jacket and puts it over the nearest chair. Mick is standing near the hallway talking to some tall guy; they look serious. The guy is talking about something, and his hands are moving around a lot. Mick's eyes move to me, he nods, and then focus back on his friend without a word.

"I'm glad you could make it," Alyssa said to me in the doorway. I could tell she wanted to say more, but I moved past her.

On the stereo, the bass is pulsing, and some guy is begging his baby to light his way. I focus and tune it out; I don't want to start thinking about music.

Spooner comes around the corner, cigar in hand, and laughing. He stops for a second, then smiles, "Hey!" he says, walking toward me. He puts the cigar in his mouth, and holds out his hand toward me. I take it, and he shakes them both with far more force than necessary. "I didn't expect to see you!" he says.

"We wouldn't let him say no," Alyssa says.

"Good," Spooner says, looking from me to her, then back to me. His eyes linger a bit on her, though; if I didn't already know better, I'd say he wanted her. Maybe he does; you never know. He lets my hand go and then puts his behind my shoulder, and walks me out of the room. As we move into the hallway, I notice that he's leading me toward a kitchen. There are some men by the sink.

As we enter, the first thing I notice is that one of them looks familiar. He's balding, skinny for his age, and his tumbler is full of clear liquid, lime on top. The other one I know for certain—he runs the garage in town. Fat guy, way too much hair. You know the type. His tumbler is full of scotch and ice. The next thing I notice is that, as soon as I walk in, they look nervously at the floor, and stop talking about whatever it was they were talking about.

"Fix you something to drink?" Spooner asks. He picks up a tumbler and looks at me.

"Vodka," I say. It's become something of a favorite of mine. The thin man takes a drink; that must be what he's drinking.

"Another, Bill?" Spooner asks the thin man, who nods. Spooner takes his tumbler. "Do you know Bill?" he asks me. I look over at the guy; I know I know him from somewhere, I just can't put my finger on it.

"No," I say.

"Bill owns a few of the Laundromats around here," Spooner says, and hands me my drink. I take a sip; this is one of the better brands—not cheap.

"Of course, you must know who this guy is," Spooner says, gesturing at the fat guy, who laughs.

"I've done alright for myself," the guy says, but it's false modesty.

"The garage over on 7th?" I ask. The guy finishes his long sip, sucks the scotch back over his teeth, and nods.

"This man is my replacement when I decide to retire," Spooner says, putting his hand on me again. I want to shake it off very badly. "It's a good thing you came tonight, actually," he says, "we're, uh—we're sort of waiting for some people to show up," he says. Immediately I get that bad feeling in my gut.

The thin guy blushes, and takes a long drink from his tumbler. The fat guy laughs in that way old fat guys have. They're all looking at me by not looking at me. "Who?" I ask.

"Oh, don't worry about it. You'll just be here to sort of keep the, uhm—the others—busy while we take care of some business," he says, looking at the other two. I set my glass down. I look at each one of them in turn.

I turn and walk out of the kitchen. The men don't follow me; they start their whispering. I'm making a straight line for the door, and Alyssa catches me. She'd been dancing to the music, but she stops long enough to try to pull me into her little world. Mick and the other guy have disappeared, and Bobby is still talking to the girls by the window.

"Come with me," Alyssa whispers in my ear as she pulls me close.

"No," I say, and try to pry free.

"Yes," she says, giggling in that low, throaty way that—I stop myself from finishing that thought. I try to pry loose again. "Come with me."

She pulls me through the door out into the yard, and then off to the side. We go behind a small fence. She rumbles around in her pocket and comes out with a sandwich bag. I already know where this is going. She holds the bag up where I can see it, shaking it and grinning. She bites her lower lip.

"No," I say, and start back for my jeep.

"Stop," she says. I don't know why, but I do. "I know who you are," she says. Something in how she says that makes my blood freeze. How could she? "I know who you are," she continues, and walks closer. Somewhere, in my mind, I know I've been through this before. My fingers ache.

"What?" I say, and try to sound annoyed, but I can't.

"You're the guy who runs from women because he's afraid," she says. My eyebrows wrinkle. "You run because someone hurt you once, and now you think that we're all going to," she says. She gets close to me, and the wind comes up from behind her. Her hair moves, and I can smell her. My fingers are throbbing, and my chest hurts.

"That's not—," I start, "that's not it."

She's already got one rolled, and she lights it. She puffs a few times, then holds some in her mouth. She grins up at me, and the moon hits her just right. Everything in me wants to run. From back inside, the singer is talking about how every poet is a thief. She exhales, and I can't help it—I grab her by the shoulders, and I kiss her.

# 28 • A Delivery

She pulls away from me, and smiles. She touches her lips with her fingers, and looks at me. Her eyes are glowing. I look around. She steps close to me, again, and wraps her arms around my neck.

"I knew it," she says.

"Knew what?" I ask.

"That you wanted me. I could tell," she says.

"I have to go," I say.

She looks at my face, then blinks and says, "Bullshit."

"I have to go," I say.

She clasps her fingers behind my head, locking her arms tighter, "Where?"

"My nephew—He'll be—," I start.

"He's not your nephew," she says.

"What?" I ask.

At that exact moment, a large car pulls up in the driveway. Some sort of limousine; a stretched out version of a truck I've seen tooling around town. It's painted white, and the windows are tinted so dark, they look like mirrors. I turn away from her, but her arms are still locked around my neck.

The back door opens. Out of it comes a man in a charcoal gray suit. He's got a black tie on, and he's wearing sunglasses. He's smoking a cigar, and his watch is gold. He looks around, then his glasses lock on my eyes. I can tell he's staring.

The front door of the house opens, and out comes Jason. He's followed by his two friends from the kitchen. They stop at the front step, but Jason goes over to the limo. I can't hear any music, anymore; I guess someone turned the stereo off. Jason shakes hands with the guy, and I get a chill down my spine. I get a picture in my head of what else is in the truck. As if on cue, three boys step out. None of them are very old, but one of them looks like he should be holding someone's hand to cross the road.

I shouldn't feel my heart racing, but I do.

"What is it?" she asks, looking at me. I wonder how she can ask that, until I remember where we're standing. She can't see the driveway; I'm blocking her.

"Nothing," I say.

"Bullshit," she says, trying to come around me. I block her. She doesn't struggle much. "What is it?" she asks.

Jason hands the guy an envelope. The guy shakes hands with him, again, and Jason turns around, leading the boys inside without saying anything to them. One looks over at me; curly black hair, brown eyes—the burning anger in them: he looks like someone else I knew, a long time ago. I hope his heel is stronger.

I try not to notice how much the men on the front step look like wolves. One of them almost looks like he's drooling. Jason looks over at me, sees me staring. He says something to the men, and they put hands on the boy's shoulders. They all walk inside, except Jason. He comes over to me.

"Hi," he says, smiling. I nod at him. He sees Alyssa. He nods to her. She unclasps her hands and straightens her hair. The music starts back up, inside.

"He gone?" I ask.

"Yeah," Jason says, his eyes drawing down into a question mark. I don't say anything.

"From New York?" I ask, motioning with my chin toward the door.

"Same stable," he says, smiling at his own little joke.

I don't.

"Well," he says, and turns around. He walks to the door, and looks back at me. He looks down and walks inside.

# 29 • A Mistake

What was that?" she asks.

"It's not important," I say, turning to walk to the jeep.

"You're leaving?" she asks.

"I don't want to be here," I say, walking.

She makes a sound in her throat.

I stop and turn a bit, "this was a mistake. I shouldn't have come," I say.

"Don't you want to—?" she asks, but stops.

I wait a moment. She looks down. I turn again, and open the door. I get in and close the door. I press in on the clutch and turn the key.

# 30 • Thrace

I turn over and see the light on his face. He looks like an Achilles when he was the same age, before he grew hate in his chest. Shorter hair, maybe, but the same nose. Something in my own chest moves just then, and I close my eyes. "Lucky boy," I say.

"What?" he whispers from the depth of near-sleep.

"Lucky. In my time, a boy as beautiful as you would have been sold at market," I say. He shifts to get the damp cloth near my face, again.

"Sold at market?" he asks.

"Yes. They'd have cut you, so you wouldn't grow anymore, and then sold you off to someone as a bed boy."

He whispers something that sounds like "they tried," but I don't ask.

After a long silence, he asks "When were you my age?"

"Long ago; long ago," I say, remembering dolphins playing in the bow waves, my father at the rudder, my mother's voice like chimes as she laughed beside me.

"How long ago?" he asks.

"I never thought much about time, then. I don't remember. I was younger than Jason, though, when he chose us for the voyage. Not the youngest, but near there," I mumble, rubbing my face with my hand.

"Who was Jason?" he asks.

"The greatest captain we had ever known. He came to Thrace only that once, but he saw me and the few others he chose from there—he said we were his secret weapon," I say, and drifted more fully off to sleep.

If I had been awake just a bit longer, I would have heard him, still deathly still, whisper "Thrace."

# 31 • Sappho's Lyre

He's sitting with his back against my knees. I'm in the chair, and he's on the floor. I'm combing his hair. My fingers ache; I never did this for her. I stop myself thinking that every stroke. I can feel his breathing through my shins. He's humming something.

"What's that?" I ask.

"Just this song," he says without turning around.

Every stroke I have to stop myself from thinking of her hair. It was nothing like his. Hers was like the sun. I stop myself.

"Where'd you hear it?" I ask.

"I dunno," he says, "nowhere. It's this lady; she calls herself Sappho. She's a lesbian, I think."

I stop combing for a second, "Sappho, huh?" I say, my mouth twitching into a grin.

"Yeah; weird, huh?" he says.

I start combing again, "What makes you think she's a lesbian?" I ask.

"I dunno—aren't all female singers who play acoustic guitars?" he asks.

I laugh, "No," I say.

"Oh," he says. I almost forget my fingers for a moment.

"What's the name of the song?"

"I dunno. Something about some guy who loved her but was too into bondage or something," he says.

"Never heard of it," I lie. I think that it's a good thing he hasn't turned around, or he'd see me smiling. These are names I haven't thought of in a long time.

"Did you ever play in a band?" he asks.

I stop brushing, "No; why?"

"I dunno—I saw your guitar—," he starts to say.

"When?" I ask. The smile falls off my face.

"I dunno," he says; he knows from the tone in my voice he shouldn't have said it.

"When?" I ask again.

He turns his head to look at me. I can't imagine how my face must look. "The other day." After a moment when I don't say anything, he goes on, "You were in the shower and I wanted to—," he starts, but trails off.

"Go on," I say.

"I wanted to wear some of your clothes," he says.

I sit back, and rest the brush on my knee. "I don't keep clothes in my closet," I say.

"I know—well, I didn't then, but I do, now," he says. His face shows that he's hoping this will end the whole discussion.

It won't. "You've never seen me go into that closet. I always get my clothes from the dresser," I say.

He doesn't say anything.

"What did you see?" I ask.

"Your guitar."

"It's in a case," I say, "You'd have had to open the case to see what was in there."

He hangs his head. He knows this has gone too far for it to come back to happy.

"I'm sorry," he says.

I stand up. He scoots forward, so that he doesn't get hit by my knee. He's cowering at my feet. His hands are up a bit; he must think I'm about to hit him. I could. At this moment, I could.

"There is a blanket and a pillow in the closet down here. In the morning I'll take you home," I say, and drop the brush. I go to the steps.

"No," he whispers.

"Goodnight," I say, and go up the steps, turning out the downstairs light as I go. He was still cowering where I left him, in the darkness, when I turn on my bedroom light and go in, shutting the door behind me. The lock's tiny click sounds like a gunshot in the silence.

# 32 • The Flood

I don't know it's a dream at the time, but I do, if that makes sense. That halfway feeling of knowing that this is not reality, but not being able to break free from the certainty of the ideas. I know you know the feeling.

I'm in the bedroom; Jacob is in bed. The lights are off. A breeze blows through the open window, rattling the blinds.

I'm moving toward the closet door. Don't ask me why. There's nothing I need in there. I put my clothes into the drawers when I moved in. The closet is for one thing only. My fingers should be aching; that's another way I can tell this isn't real.

Still, I can't stop my hand from reaching out. The knob is dull brass; the standard doorknob for an unremarkable door. I always thought that was a bit ironic—this door is completely forgettable, but what's behind it is not. The memory of the confused voices of the men around me comes back when I think of what's behind that door. The sound of the singing coming from everywhere and nowhere, and just over it the mumbles and prayers of the men.

I think about her, too. I can't stop myself. My motion toward the doorknob is taking forever, and every step bites into my memories as though they were traps springing closed. I see her face, the smile she had on our wedding day—or, I should say, the one I imagine she had, before—

Before. That'll do. That word, alone, means everything I want it to mean.

I can see her long white dress swaying in the wind behind her as she runs. I can hear the swishing of all that fabric moving over the grass. I see her gather the sides of the skirt and train into her hands and her awkward steps, trying to run in high heels. I see her drop the skirt, reaching back to hold her veil on. I see it fall, anyway.

My hand touches the knob.

I see her hand on the handle of the car door.

My hand tenses around the knob.

Her fingers clench, and the door opens.

I start to pull toward me.

She sits down behind the wheel. Just past her, I can see HIM running after her. I see how close he is. I can see in his eyes what he means to do.

The door cracks open some, revealing the darkness behind it.

She puts the key into the ignition. I see the key ring; it's a leather fob with a metal lamb on it. I gave it to her so she would feel that my chariot was hers. She turns the key, and reality seems to shudder and pulse with the engine's power.

I finish opening the door, and a flood pours out.

No guitar, just tons and tons of water, continuously pouring over me. The room is filling up, I'm sure; I can't look, though. I'm too busy trying to swim to the surface. I'm a strong swimmer. I know I can get my head above it. I struggle up and up forever, my lungs ready to burst every second. I should have made the surface by now, but I am still below water.

Eventually, I can't struggle anymore; I have to take a breath. I open my mouth, and water rushes in.

When my eyes open, Jacob is sitting up beside me. He makes no move to touch me; he knows better. For a split second, my heart goes out to him, having to watch me thrash and struggle and know he cannot do anything about it.

"Are you okay?" he whispers after a few moments.

I don't answer.

# 33 • The Furies

When he closes the jeep door, he looks through the plastic window. The bends in it warp his face, but I can still read it. I know what's there. I look away. He shoulders the backpack up higher, and turns to go. He's halfway up the stairs before he looks again. I wonder if he'll ever know how strong that makes him.

I put the jeep in gear and wheel it around the little circle at the steps of the school's entrance. As I pull up to the guard house, though, Smitty waves me down. I stop, and unbutton the window.

"Hi," he says, looking around.

"Hi," I say back.

"Listen, I know it ain't none of my business, but if I were you, I'd try to lay low for a bit," he says.

"Lay low? What are you talking about?" I ask.

"Lay low. As I say, it ain't none of my business what they were here about, but you better—," he keeps babbling.

"What are you talking about?" I ask.

"Those women," he says, looking directly into my eyes. An itch starts behind them.

"What women?" I ask, but I've got a pretty good idea.

"The women that came around here yesterday. They was looking for you," he says.

"What women? What'd they look like?"

"There were three of them; wild haircuts. Dangerous types. Suits, ties, badges. Dark glasses. New-fangled women, if you catch my meanin'. Says to me, one of 'em; 'have you seen this man,'" he says, the last part done in an accent of some sort. He's trying to imitate what she sounded like. "She sounded sorta like you, in fact," he says, as if it has just occurred to him.

"What did you tell them?" I ask.

"I says 'I ain't seen nothin', lady' and she says 'are you sure?' and whips off her glasses. I tell ya', I ain't seen eyes like that except on a wild animal; a snake or tiger or something. She looked like she was about to unhinge her jaw or somethin' and eat me."

She might have, too, if she'd thought he was lying. Luckily enough, he seems too stupid to lie. It may be the only thing that saved me.

"What else did she say?" I ask.

"Nothin', 'cept was I to see ya', she wanted I should give her a call," he said, taking a card out of his pocket. There was nothing on it but a handwritten phone number, the area code local. I look at the handwriting; like a snake, the ink even green. I look back at Smitty. "I wanted tuh thank ya'," he says, "I'm very happy," he says, looking up toward the school, and back at me.

"Good," I say without thinking about it. I put the jeep in gear, and drive off with the card.

# 34 • Supply and Demand

Jason comes in late. He's got his sunglasses on, and he's carrying his coffee. I watch him come in the front door, and go directly to the back. The woman across the counter from me notices my stare. She doesn't say anything, but she noticed. I hand her back her change. She smiles at me quickly, then leaves. I look over at Alyssa, who looks away quickly.

The phone on the desk rings. I pick it up.

"Can you come back here?" Jason asks.

"Sure," I say. I set the phone back on the cradle and walk around the counter. "Take over," I say to Alyssa. She doesn't look at me as she moves past. I walk to the back.

I knock on the door, then open it. Jason is behind his desk, and his glasses are still on. He motions me in with an impatient hand. I walk in.

"Close the door," he says. His voice is rough, dry.

I close the door and walk to the desk. I sit down and wait. He takes his glasses off, and leans forward in his chair. "How did you know?" he asks.

"About what?" I ask.

"The boy; the one who left?" he asks.

I shrug, "I asked him."

"Asked him? When?"

"When you first brought him back. I knew he wasn't going to stay," I say.

"How?"

I don't answer. He stops waiting after a moment, and looks at the desk. When he looks back up at me, I notice how bloodshot his eyes are. He hasn't slept in a while. "When was the last time you slept?" I ask.

"What?" he asks, "Oh," he says, "umm—fuck, I don't know. It's been a while."

"What happened?" I ask. I don't know that I really care, but he asked me back here for some reason. I'd like to go ahead and get it over with.

He leans back in the chair. After a minute of staring at me, he rubs his scrubs his face with his hands. He closes his eyes, and exhales, "I'm selling some things to some people for a friend, and it's getting dangerous," he says.

"Dangerous?" I ask.

"Yeah, dangerous," he says. He leans forward in the chair and moves close to me, "Just between you and me? This sort of thing is bigger than I ever guessed, y'know? Lots of moving the stuff around so that it officially gets 'lost' before it can be sold," he says. I can tell he thinks that I know what he means.

I don't know that I care enough to tell him that I don't. He's a thief; so what? "Okay," I say, "so stop doing it for a little while; let things cool off," I say.

He looks at me for a moment, then sighs, "I wish I could. Lots of demand."

Someone knocks on the office door. His head snaps around, and his eyes jerk from me to the door and then back. His breathing gets much faster. "Who is it?" he calls out.

Alyssa's voice drifts through the door, "Mr. Spooner? There's—umm—there's a kid here to see you?" she says. I can tell she thinks it's more odd than I do.

He motions from me to the door. I get up, unlock, and open the door. Just outside it, Alyssa is standing in front of a little boy. He's one of the ones from the night of the party, the one who looked so familiar. My fingers start to hurt.

"Oh," Spooner says, "my nephew. I'm sorry, I thought I'd introduced you to my nephew at the party," he says to Alyssa. The boy walks past me to the desk.

"That's all I needed," Jason says to me. I walk out, and close the door behind me.

Just as I do, I hear Spooner say "I thought I told you never to come here—"

There is a click in my mind, and I get it.

His "nephew." It became very clear what he was selling. I walked back to the counter, and stared out the window for a while.

# 35 • Thieves

The books are heavy. That's the strange thing about books; so light when it's just one or two—unliftable in more than stacks of 25. I'm carrying in the first load of the new kid's book we're going to have in the store. The boxes arrived this morning. I decided I would circumvent all the usual fighting over who had to carry them and set up the display by doing it without asking.

I set the stack down, and turn to go back for more when I notice that someone is watching me from behind the closest aisle. In the store, the stacks go one row above my head. The effect is more "library-ish," Spooner says. It's a vibe he wants; as though the books were already here—we just came along to serve them.

You'd have to hear the way he talks about it.

Whoever it is notices I've seen them, though, and moves. I go to the storeroom. As I pick up the next stack, I notice that Candace is standing in the doorway, fidgeting with her apron.

This means she wants to talk.

Since you don't have to say anything to get Candace to start when she's like this, I set the stack down and look at her. She walks forward, and does this little looking around herself thing, like some spy movie. When she finishes that, she looks at me again and, her eyes huge, says, "You're him, aren't you?"

"Who?" I ask.

"Him, *him*." she whispers as she brings a book from behind her back. Suddenly, with a sinking feeling, I know exactly what's going on. The book she pulls is an edition I haven't seen before, but I know what book it is before I read the title. This is not the first time someone has guessed. I wonder what I did that tipped her off. The front cover has a picture from some urn in black and red paint.

Naturally, whoever decided on that artwork would think "that's Greek." Of course, it isn't—it's too dark. The things people were making then didn't look like that; it comes from a later time. On the cover, in bold lettering, is that name; the name we were all saddled with—a silly name, because no one, not even then and certainly not now, ever names themselves by the boat they're on. We were always just "his crew." It's a bad title for the poem; I tried to tell the kid that but he never listened. I have to fight hard not to get lost in the flood of history that comes pouring through me.

"No, I'm not him," I say.

"No, I saw your reaction just now—you're him," she insists in her mousy way.

"No, that's Spooner's name, not mine. Did you bug him about this, too?" I ask. I'm hoping that humor will get her off the trail. Either way, I know this is one of the last days I'm working here. I'm already packing in my head.

"I don't mean *Jason*, I mean Orph—," she starts.

"Don't," I cut her off, "don't say that name."

She steps back. I must've said that more forcefully than I thought I had. She's staring at me through owl eyes. We stand there for a while, looking at each other. Her eyes go back to something resembling normal, and she puts her hand on her other elbow, holding herself. "Why are you hiding?" she asks.

"I'm not," I say.

"You're him," she says, looking at the floor.

"Why do you think that?" I ask.

"The description. It's you. It's you almost perfectly," she says.

He had always been in love with me. Most of them picked up on it. He'd only been a boy at the time; just a kid in a port town we settled in while waiting out the winter. This was before I paid much attention to them, though. He'd wanted to come to sea, but he didn't have any skill. The first time I took him out beyond the inlet, he'd been ill. We tried several times, but he always wound up sick. Then summer came, and we had to leave, and he stood on the dock, watching, and trying not to cry. I guess he'd spent most of his life pining. He'd invented half of it; just enough to turn me into something I am not. Something I never will be, no matter how long

I live. Apparently he got enough right, though.

"I don't sing or play guitar," I said.

"Lyre," she corrected.

I smiled, "Lyre," I said, "I don't play music. I don't even like music that much."

She was still looking at the floor. She had the book behind her back, like a deadly secret. I was already trying to figure out what I'd say to Jacob; if I'd say anything at all.

"I won't say anything; you don't have to worry. I just wanted to know one thing," she said. I didn't say anything. She looked up; "does that love really exist? Love that would go through the dark of the afterlife to retrieve its other half?" she asked.

I stood there, staring at her, for hundreds of years. After a while, when I knew I wasn't going to answer, I turned and walked out the back door.

I don't know how long I've got. That's the simple truth of it. If I were to say that out loud to most people, they'd nod their head according to the rules, and say "amen." Something trite like that, anyway.

They'd think I meant death.

No, I know how long I've got for that—unless something changes, I won't die. No, I meant that I don't know how long I've got in any one town before they come looking for me. I guess they haven't managed to forget about me quite yet. Every town I see them before they see me. That's a good thing. It always starts as an itch behind my eye.

The next morning, the itch starts.

I'm supposed to pick Jacob up. We're supposed to spend the night together. In his mind, I'm sure he's thinking about it right now. It's different, now. When I was his age it was men, women—age didn't matter. That was just who we were. Now, though, it's an entire identity. Men who only want to be with other men have a name and a whole list of things expected of them. Women who only want to be with men, the same.

I wonder if maybe that's not easier. If somehow, this is a solution to a problem we had then.

I remember when she was the only woman for me. When, because I had her, I didn't need any men or boys or anything else. Just her. I remember that.

The itch behind my eyes gets worse. Not long, now. Not long.

Coming down the steps, I can already tell how he feels. He's taking them two at a time, his backpack bouncing off his shoulders. His hair flops in all directions. His tiny hips seem barely enough to hold him up, and his feet look huge against his thin frame. For some reason, I smile.

He opens the door and tosses his pack inside without even looking. He waves to someone at the top of the steps.

"Who's that?" I ask, starting the jeep.

"Martin," he says, closing the door.

"Who's martin?" I ask, putting the jeep in gear.

"New kid," he says, "he knows."

"Knows what?" I ask, pulling around the driveway, and onto the road.

"About you. About the guard. He knows stuff."

My eyebrows furrow, "You told him?"

"I didn't have to," Jacob says. He's staring straight ahead, and tapping his finger against the plastic window. "He told me. He started seeing one of the mathematics professors like the same day he got here."

"What?" I ask.

"Yeah; turns out there are a bunch of professors who are like that. Martin was just getting to class, he said, and the professor just asked him out."

"Out?" I ask.

"Yeah. Like a date or whatever."

I don't say anything.

"They went out on his boat, and the guy cooked for him," he said. After a moment, he shook his head and said, "cooked for him; do you believe that?"

"How does he know about me?"

"Saw me getting things packed. He just looked at me and asked 'the guy in the jeep, right?' and I said 'yeah,'"

"What else did he say?"

"Just that he was glad."

"Glad about what?"

Jacob turns to me, and with a glint in his eyes says, "That he's found someplace where they don't frown on this sort of thing." He waits a minute, and I think of someone else I knew who did the same thing. My fingers ache. After his dramatic pause, he says "Martin says that he's been with men his whole life, and that it was scary at first, but he got used to it. He says he's been hurt a few times, but mostly not. I told him about what happened to me," he says.

"What did he say about it?" I ask.

"He shrugged. That's how we got to be friends. He didn't do that tongue-clicking thing; he didn't shake his head and say it was a shame. He just shrugged and then we went to lunch," he says, "he didn't look at me any different."

As we pull up into the parking lot in front of my apartment, a long black sedan pulls away. I see the back end as it leaves. The itching gets worse.

The door opens, and Jacob gasps. The place is trashed. The sofas overturned. The lamps on their sides. The coffee table is face down, and it's hard not to think of it as dying.

Coming into your house and finding out someone's been in it while you were away feels exactly like almost being hit by a bus. Your adrenaline starts pumping immediately, and you shake, but you're not in any danger. Jacob starts to shake.

I walk into what used to be my living room and stand there. From there, I can see the cupboards are all open, and everything is spilled out on the countertops, the floor. It looks like someone came in searching for something. I wonder what they were looking for. I wonder why they couldn't have just asked.

I was going to leave it all here, anyway.

Jacob is crying. He still hasn't moved. I turn to look at him. He's sobbing, and his bag slides from his shoulder to the floor. It lands with a thud that somehow doesn't sound right. With things rearranged, sound doesn't move the same way it did.

The place sounds alien.

"Oh, my god," he says.

I look at him. I turn and walk up the stairs. Each one creaks as if it is a part of a different staircase, in some other house.

The bedroom has been ransacked. The bed overturned, the lamps scattered. The curtains are still drawn, but with the room rearranged, the light spilling through them seems to be foreign and obscene. I hear Jacob coming up the steps. The closet is open, and the guitar is moved. Still there, but moved a bit. One of the locks is open. I hadn't opened them in so long, I wondered sometimes if they *would* open.

# 36 • Sharing History

It's a parting dinner. He doesn't know that. We had them back then. Lots of them. Part of the reason, *he* always said, to go so often is to have people make a big fuss over you all the time. Then he would smile that smile he had, the one that made us all get in Argo in the first place.

This is earlier than last time. I thought maybe I had another month, but I don't. They've already been here. This time it's not just leaving threats scrawled in blood on the door, either. They came in. They trashed the place. They were looking for me. This is somehow different than before. As if they want to end it.

So I'm leaving. Part of me wants to tell him. Wants him to know that this is the last dinner we will have together, so he can say what he wants to say. And I worry that, without the goodbye, he'll hurt himself after I'm gone. If he winds up in Hades, they might tell him the truth about me before I get there and can tell him myself. I don't want that.

"Wine," I said. He looked at me, his eyebrows making a V over his nose.

"Wine?" he asked.

"Yes," I said. I picked up the cup, and brought it to my lips. I stopped it there, though, and inhaled the delicate tang of the grapes. I swished the golden liquid around some, watching how it sparkled and caught the light. I looked over at him as I sipped; he was swirling his wine around in his cup. The sparkling wine exploded on my tongue, and then mellowed, like fire. "Wine," I said, swallowing. He sipped, and his eyes got big. Then he sputtered and coughed.

"Ugh," he said. He brought his hand to his throat, and coughed again.

"Is everything alright?" the waiter asked, passing by.

"It's just fine," I said without looking up.

"How can you drink that stuff?" the boy asked.

I sat my glass down, watching the way the lights moved around through it, like lightning. "Grapes are hard to grow; they take time and care. Even where I come from, where you can grow almost anything, grapes are picky. They always have been," I said. I picked up the glass again, and sipped. I could feel my voice slipping into the chant of the storyteller. "A grape needs constant care, you see. Like a child, almost. A grape needs to be looked after, given sunlight and shade. You can always tell what has happened to the grape when you drink the wine," I said.

"You can?" he asked, looking back down at the cup, and swirling it a bit.

"This world celebrates killers—it makes poems for the men who carry swords, but none for the men who grow grapes. The patience, the care. Where I come from, if a guest showed up on your doorstep, the first thing you did was offer him wine. Watered, of course," I said, grinning a bit, "because wine was so expensive. It still is, but then it was more. There were no supermarkets to go to; no gas station to stop off at on the way home. If you wanted wine, you had to know someone who grew grapes, someone with good barrels."

"Barrels?" he asked, bringing the cup back to his nose and sniffing.

"Yes, barrels. Wine is aged in barrels. It sits in them for years, sometimes decades. Slowly it takes on the taste, the character of the wood that it is stored in. The grapes, like people, stretching into themselves because of where they grow up. Wine is *aged*, you see—it's supposed to be old when you drink it. It has to have time to gel, to become what it is. Again, like children. You have to give it a good place to grow up. Even then, this was true. The wine you poured for your guest became what people thought of you. Where I came from, you would feast a guest for days on end before even asking his name; you would discuss the weather, drink to his health, all without knowing anything about him other than that he was alive—the wine celebrated that fact. During that time, your guest would want for nothing. In my home, we watered the wine, but it was good to start with, so it stayed good. My father knew a man who grew grapes and olives on a huge tract of land near the ocean," I said, and felt myself slipping off. My fingers ached. I stopped myself, "Here, in this country, you pour coffee. You value the bold taste of the burned bean. Then, though, it was the grape." He was staring at me, and then he took a sip. His face didn't distort, this time. "The grape you were drinking at your hosts table had been through the same drought as you five summers before. It had been a tiny bud on a vine the year you were born. Wine is alive in a way that nothing else is—it is history bottled."

The boy looked at me, his face quiet, his eyes listening. "This wine we are drinking is strong, unwatered. It would have been served by someone very rich, very powerful. An island king, perhaps, just before he went off to war—just before he decided the fate of the world." I picked up the bottle, and read the year off the label out loud. "That was the year this bottle was corked, and put away. That was the year this bottle started to grow—what were you doing that year?" I asked. I could see he was thinking, and he sipped again. This time his lips curved upward a bit at the taste. "This kind of grape takes five or six years to grow full enough to be ready to harvest. Subtract five or six years from the year it was bottled—what were you doing that year? What was happening in the world?" I asked. He reached for the bottle, and looked at the label. He poured himself more, and moved to set the bottle back in the bucket.

"You've just made a grave mistake, young lordling," I said, smiling.

"What?" he asked, stopping.

"You reached for the bottle; that means you must be the host. I am the guest, and you are the host. If you are the host, then you don't just see to your own needs at the table. You must," I said, reaching for his hand, and guiding it over to my glass. I tipped his wrist, so that he poured the wine into my glass, "see to the needs of your guests," I said. When it had filled most of the way, I let go of his wrist, and he stopped pouring. "When you are the lord of the house, and the guest is drinking the wine you serve, you want to show off that wine; to show off how unwatered it is, how generous you are," I said, smelling the wine and drinking again. "You want to show that you are sharing the history of your land, of your people—*your* history with your guest."

Later, we're lying arm against arm, both panting.

"I can still feel you inside me," he says. He's said this before, but tonight I think he means more. It's what I wanted; for him to know in some physical way that I was leaving. "Will you help me more next week. Like you did with Homer. We're reading the *Aeneid*." He's turned his face toward me, and rolled slightly in my direction. I don't look, because his body, when it's like that...so like a woman's. I would get confused, and we'd touch again, and then I might not leave. I wouldn't be much help with that one; I never knew the kid. I mean, I met him after. By then, though, he was already a man and had adoring fans of his own. Then they sent him away. Something he did to one of his pupils, I heard. I read it, though.

"It's about leaving," Jacob says.

"What?" I ask.

He pulls his body closer. I feel his warmth against me. He stretches a leg over mine.

"That's what the teacher said; that it was a story about leaving. About people who always have to leave places that they could call home very easily because they are searching for home. Diaspora, he says."

If there was one thing we excelled at in the time before this one, it was knowing how to leave.

# 37 • Time and Tide

The drive back to the school is long, and quiet. He still doesn't realize that this is the last time we'll be seeing each other. I keep thinking about him; wondering what his life will be like. He doesn't seem like the type that will hurt himself. Most of them haven't. Almost all of them go on to write books. I think that maybe he will, too. Though, in his case, it won't just be some angst-driven thing.

I think Jacob will write an important book.

As we pull past the guard shack, I notice no one is there. People are up on the steps, moving in and out of the building. Cars in the parking lot. But no one at the guard shack. I pull the jeep to a stop.

"I'll call later, after classes," he says. I want to kiss him good bye. I want to tell him. But I don't. He opens the door, and I hear his sneakers thud on the pavement. He closes the door. The thick plastic of the window warps his face some. He cocks it to the side and smiles. I put the jeep into gear and start away.

This never gets any easier.

Normally, I'd have already put the guitar into the jeep. I'd have left for the interstate right after I dropped him off at the front of the building. Clean.

I didn't this time, though. I don't know why.

The itching is maddening behind my eyes. I know this is a mistake, but I think there's enough time. I also have to stop in and get the last check. There was a time when I didn't need cash to move around. Now, there's no way to do it without. I should have done all this ahead of time.

They're close.

When I walk in, Candace is behind the register.

"Hi," I say.

"Hi," she says, not looking up. I can tell she's still thinking she knows who I am.

"Check?" I ask.

"Back with Mr. Spooner," she says.

Somehow, I knew it. I knew this wasn't going to go smoothly. "Thanks," I say, and walk toward the back. I want her to have him bring it out, so I can stay near the windows; to watch the parking lot.

"Hey," Mick says as I walk by the aisle he's stocking. I stop. Everything in me screams to just keep walking; to get out as fast as I can. The itching is so powerful, I want to claw at my eyes. But I don't. If there's one thing I've learned about goodbyes after so many of them, it's that people will do anything to delay you leaving if they know you're going. So I have to act like nothing is unusual.

"Hi," I say.

"New translation," he says, holding up a book. I laugh a little at how things reoccur in our lives, turning up over and over again. "Do you know it?"

"I know the poem; I didn't know the poet," I say.

He laughs, "I knew you would. You're like that."

"Like what?"

"You—you know things," he says. I start to go.

"Listen," he says, leaning against the rack. I stop. "I was wondering if maybe sometime you'd like to go get some coffee."

"I can't," I say, only half turning back to him.

"Oh," he says, "well, if you're not—I mean I'm sorry if you aren't. I just thought that, y'know—,"

I stop him by putting my hand on his shoulder. I smile. "That wasn't 'no.' Just 'I can't,'" I say.

His brows furrow. I squeeze his shoulder just a bit; he's warm, compact. That inbetween place of softness of voice, but also tough sinew. Men like him spend so much time preparing for war in gyms, making their bodies hard. Their world makes them like this; always having to disguise the soft under the muscle as if invaders would come over the walls tomorrow. But the magic they have is in the soft; the moment when one warrior touches another and the armor is peeled away. As if on cue, he does this.

"He's not really your nephew, is he?" he asks.

I'm leaving, now, so there's no reason to lie, "No," I say.

He nods, looking down.

I turn and go. There was more I wanted to say, like 'you'll find the man you're looking for, don't give up.' Because this world is going to try to get him to settle. To settle for one man because they want him under control. To settle for a life that mimics the lives of those who want to stay with the same person forever not because it's who they love, but because they are afraid of being alone. And he'll do fine, this one, even in a world that doesn't understand how valuable someone like him is.

Spooner is in his office, the door slightly cracked. He thinks this gives him an air of mysterious power. That people see the half-closed door and think twice before bothering him. This is the way that people in this time think about power.

I push the door open. I'm not afraid for him to see me as I am; not now.

"Ah, there you are," he says. He picks up the envelope. He's sad, I can tell. He hands it over to me, and I take it, but at the last second he doesn't let go. This is what I was talking about: even with me not saying goodbye, this is how they delay you when they can sense you're off.

"I have to go," I say.

"We should talk," he says.

"I have to go," I say.

"Then I'll be blunt: I'm going to retire," he says. "And I want you to take over. I've already started the paperwork, all you need to do is—,"

"No," I say.

"What?" he says. I can tell this isn't for show. He really thought I was going to stay here the rest of my life. He thought I was like him.

"No," I say.

"I don't understand. This is a golden opportunity for—,"

"Candace," I cut him off. "She wants it, and she'll do well. But I have to go."

"But she's just a kid."

I shake my head, "No, she isn't. All this time she's been here, right under your nose, and you couldn't see it because you're not looking. All of these people, they're incredible," I say, surprised at how vehement this is all coming out. "But you're not paying attention. You're too worried about what you want to see them. You tell them what to do but don't see that they already know. And that they have ideas. Powerful ideas. Talk to them," I say, turning to go, "and give it to Candace."

As I'm leaving, I hear him lean back in his chair.

I hope he listened.

## 38 • Potential

**W**hat was your dad like?" Jacob asks.

One of those nights where the room smells of us after. He's lying against me, his arm around my chest. Some part of me registers that she used to lay like this, too, but I refuse to let it get to the surface.

"He was very tall," I say, "an important man. I don't remember much of him."

"And your mother?" he asks.

I sigh and put my hand in his hair. "A writer. She was always writing something, and talking about how inspiring things were."

"My mom was nice, too. My dad was..." he says, drifting off.

"Was what?" I ask.

It's unusual for me to ask, but I'm relaxed. He shifts a bit, nestling in tighter. "He was convinced he was a prophet. One of those guys who has direct messages from God."

I let that stand for a while.

"I ran away and got into a lot of trouble. I told you about that, right?" he asks.

He has. It makes me feel terrible. Like I maybe should have been there for him.

"My dad died in his sleep. Heart attack, they told us. Turns out he had this huge life insurance policy. So now I get to go to this school. Mom gets to live in Europe like she always wanted. She says she's thinking of teaching. I didn't even go to the funeral. I don't know if anyone did."

"One day," I say, not knowing why I'm telling him this, "when I was very little, a relative of my mother's came by. He was a famous doctor and musician. He recognized...I don't know...something in me. A potential. Something my father would never have seen. He was grooming me to take over for him. A line of work I'd never be any good at. But my mother's relative, he said I could be great. So he gave me a gift and taught me how to play. I can't describe how it was—the notes just made sense. I felt them with my whole body. I practiced every day until my fingers bled. Then I would put paste over them and play more. It seemed like...like the world only made sense when I was playing."

"So you *do* play music," he said, shifting up on his elbow so he could look me in the face.

"No," I say.

"But you just said—,"

"That was a long, long time ago."

# 39 • Lessons

Oree?" he heard a woman's voice call. He rolled his eyes, and hugged his dirty knees closer to his body. Below, the waves crashed against the cliff.

Only his mother called him that. And in all of Thrace, there was no other person that he least wanted to talk to. Thrazeus left to go home hours ago, but he could still feel fingers on him, lips pressed to his. All he wanted was to stare out into the ocean, watching the sails come and go. His mother would want something ridiculous like washing the steps before company came.

"Oree," came the voice again. Less of a question this time; more impatient. Soon, she'd send Thag, the servant they'd recently bought. Though her voice was sweet, and sounded like chimes in a breeze, he hated the sound of it.

He sighed, knowing that his time for simply sitting, simply being, was coming to an end. After the dinner last night, he and Thrazeus had gone off to a far corner of a forgotten hall. From there, they could see the small temple to Apollo. He'd watched Thrazeus, as he always did secretly, slip out of his tunic and settle against the cushions they'd dragged with them. It wasn't until he felt fingers lightly gliding on his back that he though perhaps Thrazeus had been watching him, too.

He stood up, and slid back into his sandals, hating how soft his feet had become. He'd never even thought about it until Thrazeus had entered his life. Their family was a bit more backwoods, and they didn't wear shoes or water their wine. They were tall and wide and happy. Thrazeus was always climbing something or stalking something through the underbrush.

"Oree!" his mother's voice came on the wind. He sighed, and wondered how it always seemed to be able to find him no matter where he was, no matter how far away. He started for home. The sound of the crashing waves diminished, but he thought he heard one last deep crash saying "soon."

The house was in motion when he arrived; day laborers had been purchased. Rugs were being beaten, steps were being washed. He'd never seen such a thing before.

"Where have you been?" his mother demanded as he walked onto the front greeting porch.

"Away," he answered, surly. He tried to keep walking past, but her hand grabbed his arm. She frowned.

"A relative of mine is coming; he's—he's very important, Orpheus. I want you to go to the spring and wash yourself. Leave your clothes here; they're filthy. I'll have someone clean them," she said. Her eyes were on fire. He had seen her like this before, but only about the speeches she'd written for father. She'd get demon-eyed like this as she listened to him speak the words she'd worked over in front of the men of the town, mouthing the words along with him as he spoke, sometimes wincing in pain if he hit the wrong note.

"Fine," he said, walking away. Her hand slid from his arm as he moved.

Inside, though, he was excited—for her to be this worked up, it must be someone very important who was coming. That meant the best food. His uncle was probably out hunting for boar at this very moment! If he hurried getting his bath, he could be back in time to see them do the slaughter. He stripped out of his clothes and went sprinting along the path to the spring.

The water was incredibly hot against his skin. He hadn't realized how dirty he'd become since his last bath until the grime was washed away and the pink, smooth skin was revealed below. He dipped his head under, waiting a moment before coming up. He listened to his heart thrum in the empty deep of the spring pool. Like a war drum. He came back up and sat on the small, flat stone his mother had one of the laborers drop in a few weeks back. He leaned back, and felt the moment.

He closed his eyes and started humming to himself. It wasn't any song in particular, more like one he made up—the notes that existed between the notes of some of the other songs he'd heard.

First one phrase, and then the reverse of that phrase. Next a close relative of that phrase, then a distant echo of that relative. Like questions and answers that brought new questions; a conversation among geniuses. He was naked in the warm water, eyes closed, floating in the music brought to life.

"Mind if I join you?" a man's voice asked.

His eyes snapped open and he stopped singing. The man was tall, lean, with the hard muscles of use. He had long, flowing blonde hair which was enough to make the boy curious about where the man had come from. He was dirty, and carried a longbow with him. A professional hunter, then, maybe? Or a soldier?

"You may," the boy answered, using the voice his mother had taught him to use with strangers who might not know what an important household he came from.

"No need to stop singing on my account," the man said. He slid out of his clothes and set them down near his bow and arrows. When he slid into the water, quite a bit of grime came off him, too.

"Was I singing?" the boy asked.

"Oh, yes. And not too horribly, I might add. Who taught you to sing so nicely?"

"No one," he answered.

"Hmm," the man replied, and leaned his head back with a sigh.

"Are you a soldier?" the boy asked.

"No," the man replied without opening his eyes.

The boy looked him over again. The long hair, the hard physique; he was like a walking statue. "A hunter, then?"

A smile played at the corners of the man's mouth, "you might say that."

Silence stretched between them. The man seemed to be asleep, while the boy watched him slyly. Eventually, because it was his habit while bathing, Orpheus fell back to humming. After a time, he was back to weaving complex patterns. Then he became aware that some of the answering phrases that were coming back to him weren't what he was humming. Another voice had joined him. He opened his eyes to find the man, still relaxed, with eyes closed, humming along. For every phrase he set loose, the man answered and in the answer, there was another questioning phrase. They were weaving their separate musics together like a tapestry. In his awe of it, the boy drifted silent again.

"Why stop, little bird?" the man asked, opening his eyes for the first time in what seemed like years. He was smiling.

"I need to go," the boy said.

"So soon?"

"We are expecting company," he said, climbing out of the pool.

"Ah, a large feast, then?"

"I'm sorry I can't invite you; I don't know your place, or his."

"It is proper that you wouldn't want to dishonor your guest by possibly inviting such a rogue as myself," the man said, laughing, closing his eyes again. "Very well, off with you."

He walked back along the trail to the house, thinking of how only one other thing had ever compared to how exciting it was to sing with someone else. There had been something bigger than them hovering between. Their bodies hadn't mattered, anymore.

Coming down the path to his home, he saw the servants in chaos. The hour his mother liked to serve formal dinners to friends of his father would not come for quite some time. There had never been a formal dinner for any of her relatives. In fact, he tried to remember the last time any of her relatives had ever come, and to his surprise found he couldn't. In the last 10 years, no one from her family had ever come.

He went to his room. They'd put down fresh straw, and he could smell the new oil in the lamps. A new set of clothes had been put out, much finer than anything they'd ever made him wear for guests of his father. He slid into them, feeling the cloth against his skin. New oil had also been put out for his hair. Thericius came in quietly, and the boy sat down. The somewhat older boy began to braid the other's hair, dabbing the oils through it as he went. The boy had often wanted to talk to the slave, to ask him about his life before coming to their household, and about his home, but he never had. His mother had a strict rule about such things.

They both heard the haunting melody coming down the hall before they saw anyone in the doorway. Thericius finished with the boy's hair and stepped away to the wall. Melius swept into the room, singing as she always did. Of course, like Thericius, her name was not Melius. She'd had another name in the far off country that the slavers had taken her from. Her skin was a rich brown, and her hips moved to a continuous rhythm, even when she was standing still. She lived inside a song. Though the boy could never admit it to anyone, he was entranced with her.

She said something in a language he didn't understand, then motioned for him to stand up. As he did she inspected the clothing, adjusting it here or there. Then she inspected the hair, running her hand over it lightly. She pulled a small white shell with a band attached to it from the folds of her gown. She slid it on to the end of his braid. In broken Greek, she sent Thericius off to fetch a bottle from her room.

She turned his hands over to inspect under his nails. He hadn't thought to clean them, so they were still a mess. She shook her head and then pulled a small bone tool from her gown. Where his mother would have gouged and scraped, though, she delicately guided the tool under the nails. He looked up into her face as she worked, listening to her hum a song that repeated itself, coiling tightly, then releasing one step further, then coiling again only to take one more step away.

Thericius returned with the bottle just as she finished the last finger. She took the bottle and put some of the oil just under his chin, and on the lowest part of his back. He smelled oranges. Thericius brought his good sandals to the boy, as well, which were kept only in his mother's room so he wouldn't forget and wear them out playing. She disliked how far he roamed during his play hours, but far more than that how often he would destroy his clothing while away.

Melius stood back and looked at him. Again, she said something in a different language. Then she said "Prince," and ushered Thericius out of the room with her as she left.

"Oree?" his mother called, as if she knew Melius had finished just that precise moment.

He looked himself over one last time, and found he didn't recognize himself at all this way. He found his mother in the front hall. She gestured him over to her, and positioned him just in front of her, her hands resting on his shoulders. Past the orange smell of the oil Melius had put on him, he could smell his mother. It was different; wild, like nothing he'd smelled before. No one else was there; no servants, none of father's men with their bright shields. Just the two of them.

"This man is a cousin of mine, Oree, and he must be treated with the utmost respect," she nearly whispered, which was quite odd for her.

"Who is he?" the boy asked.

Before she could answer, a man appeared at the far end of the path leading to the formal entrance. "One knee," she said. She bent down, and bowed her head. He was too stunned to follow suit—he'd never once seen his mother anything but regal and defiant. Before he could mimic her position, the man was at the steps.

"Well, little bird," the man called in recognition.

It was the man from the springs.

His mother stood, putting her hand on his back. "My lord," she said.

The man laughed and came up the steps. The boy was further stunned; he had not been asked into her presence, but had simply strolled up the steps.

"And this little bird must be—,"

"My son, lord," she said. "We named him Orpheus."

"Orpheus," he said, and smiled, as if the word meant something more to him than merely a name.

"Yes, lord," she said.

"Enough with titles. Soon enough, if I have my way, I will be your brother-in-law," the man said. As before, though his clothing was clean and very richly dyed, he carried nothing other than his marvelous long bow. His hair flowed free, and seemed to glow in the sun.

"Welcome into my home," she said. She gestured for him to precede her inside. He walked in, and though he could have sworn it was there a moment before, the boy noticed that the bow had disappeared. In his awe, he must've not seen it handed to one of the servants, he thought. "Wine," she said out loud to no one in particular. Servants appeared and set a feast on the formal dinning table. The man went to the head of it immediately, and sat down. His mother sat to the man's right.

"Orpheus, this is a relative of mine, Apollo." The boy stopped in mid-step, nearly falling over.

"You hadn't told him?" the man asked.

"Not yet," she said.

"Hmmm," he said, a smile playing at the edges of his lips. "Come, boy, sit at my side while your mother and I talk."

He obeyed, but was still too stunned to say anything. *The Apollo?* He could not be. It could not be. That would mean that—

"It seems my visit has forced you to tell him before you were ready. For that, I apologize, little bird," the man said to his mother.

She poured wine for all three of them. She sipped her cup.

"May I tell him, then?" the man asked. Something in his air said that he was going to whether she agreed or not. She consented, though. "Your mother, little bird, inspires poets and singers. The best of them, in fact, of those who sing of the deeds of great gods and men. She and her sisters are those who bring us art," he said.

"We merely inspire, cousin," she said.

"My brother was also so infatuated with her that—," he began to say.

"I think that would be perhaps more than he needs to know," she said, cutting him off. The man laughed. It was such a pure, musical sound that the boy couldn't help but join in, though he was utterly confused.

"Well, suffice it to say, then, that she found she liked a meek sort of man rather than a warlike one, and settled down here, in Thrace, with your father." The boy felt there was something of an insult in all of that, but couldn't put his finger on it.

"Who is also a great man," she said.

"Perhaps. As far as men go, at any rate," the man said.

"Food?" she asked, and motioned for servants to come. He waved them away.

"Tell me, little bird; what are your plans for him," the man asked, putting a hand on the boy's shoulder. "Off to war to be slaughtered for some fat thief's greed? Tell me, boy, is that what you want?"

"There are many great deeds to be done in war," she said as she adjusted her skirts.

"Yes. Dying and bleeding and losing limbs—many great deeds," the man said while rolling his eyes.

"Perhaps, Oree, you'd like to go and make sure the dinner is coming along?" she asked, her eyes telling him to go. He began to rise to his feet, but the man's hand pushed him back down, again.

"No, let the boy stay. He's a handsome fellow, and I've little enough beauty to look upon in the days ahead."

"What is your errand?" she asked.

The man chuckled, took a long gulp of wine, and wiped his mouth on the back of his hand. "I've just come from seeing a woman," he said. "Here," he said and his other hand put a lyre on the table, "play, boy."

The boy hadn't seen him bring the instrument in. A thrill ran up the boy's spine, like lightning had just run through the room. "He doesn't know how," his mother said.

"What?" the man asked.

"He doesn't—," she repeated.

"I know what you said," the man said, his tone going cold. "I just don't know that I believe it. Why would you not—?" he began and then stopped. "Swords, instead?" the man asked.

My mother blushed. She looked at me and then at him, then back at me.

"Well, you may not be able to stand up to the man, but I certainly will. Come, boy," the man said, standing. He picked up the lyre and stood next to the bench. The boy didn't know what to do.

"His father wants him trained as a warrior king," she said.

"He is half yours," the man said.

"And half his father's," she said. Her voice was gentle, but it cut the air like a whip.

The man leaned in, and though his face never changed from a calm, benevolent smile, I could tell he was dangerous. "And. Half. *Yours*. He is no mortal man doomed to butcher other men simply so his father will smile down upon him. Pretending that he is will only lead all involved to misery." He put his hand under my arm and helped me to stand. "Now I know why you have not taken him to Delphi for me to see, for your father to know. I've been sitting here this whole time wondering why I can't remember what I told the women about your son and now I know why—you haven't brought him yet."

"His father did not wish it," she said, looking only at the tabletop.

The man stood all the way up; maybe it was because I was standing so close, but he felt much taller than he had been. He then turned to face me, and put both hands on my shoulders. His eyes seemed to bore through me, and I could have sworn they went white as stone.

"No!" my mother said, standing. From the corner of my eye, I saw that she made no move to stop him.

The room grew icy. Then his eyes returned, and the room seemed oppressively warm. "Ah," he said, as if he knew something we did not.

"What did you see?" she asked.

He turned us both for the doorway, and I knew from the pressure of his hand I was to walk with him.

"What did you see?" she asked, following us.

He stopped, holding me where I was with one hand. Over his shoulder he said, "Interested in his future now, are you?" Then he walked me out of the house.

I don't remember anything else for the next month or so, except music. The pain in my fingers that brought forth joy. Music, and the warmth of his arm around me in the night.

I look over and Jacob is asleep. I knew he would be. Sometimes I like that he's that predictable. I reach over him and shut the light off. The blackness rushes in, and then fades slowly to a gentle blue. The light in the courtyard outside comes through the leaves of the tall tree outside the window and make patterns across his face. He seems like a puzzle.

For a moment, I think about the first boy I met coming back from one of the endless number of wars. In his face, I could see the boy I remembered leaving a year earlier, but behind his eyes only endless trenches. I remember how his face contorted, and he laughed bitterly as he pulled a volume of poetry from his backpack. "Keats," he said, as if it was a bad word. The next day, he disappeared for a while. He came back smelling of wood smoke, with soot on his jacket, and that book had disappeared.

And I think about how much she had liked a particular ode to Apollo that one of the temple poets had composed. She had asked for it every time we were close, and the boy who wrote it not too busy.

My fingers ache.

I look to the closet. The door is slightly open, as it always seems to be. And I'm tired of resisting. I want to hear the songs of home. I wish there were someone else to play them for me, but mine are the only fingers that remember.

I shift him, so that he rests on a pillow. He moves a bit, then settles back in. I get up out of the bed as quietly as I can. I stand there, in the dark, unmoving, between bed and closet for a long time. On the bed, he moves a leg, and his ankle pops loudly in the silence. I reach out and move the door open. On the shelf, I can see the shape. The metal gleaming from the tiny light of the lamp outside the window. The leaves make a puzzle pattern on the case.

"Mmm," he moans in his sleep.

My arm stays locked around him for quite a while. I know the instant the music erupts from it, I will feel home once more. That I will remember her, with all the release that will follow from that. That I will lose myself in the missing and not have to run, anymore. All I have to do is touch it just once, and then I can let go.

"Mmm," he moans, again. My head turns. His dreams are often bad if I am not near. He's curled himself into a ball.

I close the closet door. I climb back into bed as quietly as I can. I shift him, so that his head is on my chest. He uncurls slowly. I mark the time, the long rests marching steadily, by one by one. I wish there were someone to play the songs of home for me.

I wish mine were not the only fingers left that remembered.

# 40 • Lover

The sun is starting to come up. Through the curtains I can see the bluish light. It seems like the entire time I've known him, this has been my relationship with Jacob. Him sleeping, me watching the sun rise and listening to him breathe.

When Jacob retells this story, I wonder what he'll say; if people will understand. I'm so old, now, that I don't care much. This is merely curiosity. I wonder if they'll understand that he was never a child—not the way that he came up. Like the Spartans with their dog pits, this one was bound to be a warrior from the beginning. I guess that's what makes all of this okay for me, in my own head.

Somewhere, they're searching. The feeling has gone from merely dread to acceptance. I don't think they've ever been this close, before. I watch the blue light slowly outline his legs, his shoulders, and I know that this has to be our last night together, me and him. In a while I'm going to get up, fix coffee, and chastise him for being late like I always do. Then I'm going to drop him off and wave as if nothing has changed. I'll come back here, get the bag out from under the bed, and then drive away. If I know them, they'll track me to him, see that I'm not there, and then quietly leave.

"Lover," my wife says, gently. And I bolt awake. I look around the room quickly. Jacob is still asleep, but moved off of me to one side of the bed. Other than him, the room is empty. My eyes scan every inch of it. I must have drifted to sleep; the sun has gone from blue to white and streams through the curtains intently.

I slide out of bed quietly. Down the stairs silently, searching every bit that I can see. I stand in the middle of the living room.

She's not here.

# 41 • Something Just For Us

I knew his name, you see. That's what made everything that came after much harder. I knew who he was. I knew that he was already married, and had children. But you see, he wandered. He could go anywhere he wanted and say he was there to "civilize" them; invent a new him for every new town. And people, they ate it up. They wanted to be more *civil* than the next town over, so they took him in. 'Please teach us how to keep bees,' they would say; 'please show us how to make cheese.'

He took to calling himself Aristaeus. "The Best." As if that shouldn't have been the only warning anyone needed.

I didn't stop him, though. That's where it went wrong. I still had faith in people, then. We hadn't been back from the voyage long. Jason had moved on to other things—none of us saw him much. With him gone, we all kind of drifted away, too. I was busy trying to figure out how to win *her*.

Saying her name was almost like saying "you're the sea" in English. In my mind, it was just like that first time seeing the sea. Not the first time ever seeing, but the first time *seeing;* the first dawn on the open ocean. No sailor ever forgets that image—the horizon has never seemed so close, and yet so far for him. And she was like that. Most of the poets who wrote about her kept calling her a wood nymph, either as a dirty pun or through misguided religion, trying to get her to sleep with them. That was what first drew his attention to her, I know. What good would all his cultivation be if he couldn't have a tame pet nymph to show for it? For him, she was just another field to plow and plant.

I had tried to talk to her several times when we first returned home. I was wild, then. Impressed with myself. After all, wasn't I the one who had saved my crew? Didn't I deserve to be hailed as a hero?

Such is the nonsense of boys.

The rest of the boys, they all chased after her, but in that way that they have—half crazed and not concentrating. For most of them, she was just another girl to be pursued. For the other half, she was a convenient topic of midnight conversation to get the first half aroused enough to agree to let them go down on them. Again, such is the nonsense of boys. But I'd been around the world. I knew what was out there, and I knew that she was the best of it.

I don't remember anymore exactly why I decided that day was the particular day that I was going to introduce myself to her, but I remember waiting specifically for that day. Aristaeus was giving one of his grand speeches again, and he'd drawn a crowd. She was at the outer edge with another girl, one of her friends. I had been sidling up to her from the other end of the crowd for what seemed like hours. Finally she looked up at me, and our eyes met. It was every cliché that people put into movies—worlds stopping, swelling music, all of it. Her eyelids closed down a bit, and the edges of her mouth quirked. Then she looked away and smiled.

"Hello," I said.

"Hello yourself," she said without looking up. Then she looked back at Aristaeus.

"Listen, I was wondering if you'd maybe like to—," I was saying, looking at my feet.

"Yes," she said.

"—but I'd understand if you didn't, I mean," I kept on. I was so convinced she wouldn't want anything to do with me that I hadn't heard her say yes. Then it dawned on me. "Oh," I said, then the full realization hit me, "Oh!" I looked up, and our eyes met again.

"I have to take some bread that's almost finished baking to my friend's mother by the beach," she said. With that, I looked around for her friend, and saw that she had moved off a few feet. "You may accompany me."

"I'm—," I was saying.

"I know who you are," she cut me off.

"Oh," I said.

And that was how we met. Everyone else treated me as if I might bite at any moment, but she never once showed fear. I followed her back to her house that afternoon, and walked with her while she carried bread to her friend's mom. Over the next week or so, she kept finding little errands she needed to do each day, and would ask me to escort her. It didn't take long for people to notice that she and I were always together.

At the end of that first week was the first time she asked me to play for her. We found a little clearing not far from the beach that night. I started off with one of the up tempo songs for dancing, but she stopped me. Put her hand right on the strings, over the top of my fingers. "No," she said, her voice going low and soft, "something just for us." So I played a slow one, one that Jason had liked so much while we were out on the open ocean and the stars were shining down on us, a lullaby my mother had taught me. She closed her eyes, and tilted her chin up, nodding her head just slightly in time. The second chorus came around, and I leaned in and kissed her. Even then, I thought she might push me away, but she didn't. Like everyone, I'd been with other boys, other girls, but that was the first time I'd ever made love to anyone.

We were to be married a week later. Her family was devout in their worship of Athena at home. I held to the gods as a good man should, but never had picked out one special one above all others, so we decided to have the priestess of Athena do the ceremony. In keeping with the ritual, we hadn't seen each other for a few days. Her family kept her sequestered, and would have one of her youngest brothers send me her notes.

What I didn't know at the time was that Aristaeus wasn't at all happy about the news. That he had a few boys that craved his attentions dogging her brother's every step. That they were threatening to beat him up if he didn't show them the messages, that they would then copy and take back to Aristaeus.

I didn't know any of this until I was called to come to her home by her youngest brother. He came to my door and knocked like a madman. I opened it and smiled to see him, until I saw that he was beaten. "What happened?" I asked.

"They took it and told him," the boy cried out hysterically.

"What?" I asked

"The boys, they beat me up and took the note," he said, collapsing into a little ball.

"What boys?" I asked, kneeling down.

"The ones that work for Aristaeus," he managed to get out after some false starts.

In an instant, somehow, I understood what was going on. I picked him up and put him down on the bench in front of the table. "Stay here," I said, and I grabbed my sword.

When I got to her house, he was at the front door. He looked as if he'd been in a fight, himself; torn and bloody. Nearby, I could see her oldest brother, the poet, knocked unconscious. I checked to see if he was breathing still. He was, so I turned my attention back to Aristaeus.

"What is this about?" I asked. I already knew, but I wanted him to say it.

"You have no right to her!" Aristaeus said, turning to face me.

"That is for her to decide," I said. I saw his eyes go from mine to the sword and back.

"You're just a brute; an uncivilized stinking warrior—what could you possibly give her?" He was practically mad; tears were welled in his eyes. His fingers were curled like claws.

"What is it *you* think you could give her that I could not?" I asked.

Something about the way I asked must have been the final straw. He lunged at me, and I caught him by the hair. My sword was seconds from going through his neck when she screamed. I held him there like that and looked. She had come out of the gate and was standing there, her hands covering her mouth. "Stop!" she yelled.

I looked back at him. I flung him away by his hair. Don't think of it as some act of bravery, or of better angels. Had I know what would happen later, I'd have run him through and fed him to boars. He crouched there, crying. Her little brother came along just then and told me everything; the copied notes, the threats—everything. I don't know what was worse, realizing that a figure so many people believed in was so twisted inside, or that he simply crouched there the entire time listening and sobbing.

She hadn't known, either. I watched her face as she listened to how he'd been following her, gaining every little bit of information he could about her, reading all of her letters to me and mine to her.

"What do you want me to do?" I asked her.

"Just let him go," she said. That was her, I thought, as he got up and walked away. She could forgive anyone anything, even him.

That was part of the problem, though. We forgot about him. Over the next few days, we went about planning our wedding, and we forgot about him. The day finally came, and I was ready. Her eldest brother, the poet, was standing by my side. All of the others from the voyage had long ago departed for their own corners of the world, so he was the closest thing I had. His face had healed nicely, and I could see how her mother beamed to see him in fresh clothes with his hair oiled. The priestess looked powerful and solemn in her robes, and the sun was just ducking behind the wine-dark sea. It was perfect.

Then came the horrible screaming. I raced through the crowd until I found her. When I got to her she was already swelling up from the venom. She'd managed to wander far enough away from where she'd been bitten that I could get to her, but from where we were I could see the ground writhing back where the nest must have been.

She was already dead.

Her friend who had been her maiden in waiting that day finally managed to get out the story, later. Aristaeus had burst in to the house and tried to take her by force. He'd hired a ship and planned to whisk her away to a wedding he'd set up. He'd been babbling about all of this as he tried to force Eurydice from the house. Her friend had clung to him to get him to stop, and it had been just enough to allow her friend to get away. Aristaeus had knocked her to the ground, and then chased after.

Dressed normally, she had always been surefooted. However, in a long robe with nothing to protect her feet, and afraid, she hadn't been looking very carefully. The maid had gotten there just in time to see Aristaeus chasing Eurydice toward a place where the family had been stacking wood for the bonfires at the banquet after the ceremony. She said it looked for a moment like Eurydice merely tripped, but then came the awful screaming and the hissing. A nest of snakes had taken up residence in the pile. Not seeing, she had run right through them, and they had lashed out at the intrusion. Aristaeus had stopped instantly, she said, and as if understanding exactly what would happen after, ran.

And my wife was dead.

In the dark, listening to Jacob breathe, I thought about the wedding song I'd written just for her. I thought about how I had never played it. How I'd never even hummed it, again.

As if miles away, in some distant land, my fingers ache.

# 42 • No Fortune

It wasn't like there hadn't been signs.

We had ordered in Chinese. This was at the beginning of summer. We were both sitting in the apartment with the window open. Someone's chimes across the way were ringing out long, clear notes.

I was eating slowly, but he'd already finished his, and he went for the bag.

"Here," he said. He pulled out two fortune cookies. He handed me one, and got that look on his face like he expected something of me. I set my chopsticks down. He took the other cookie and cracked it open. "You are a generous spirit...*in bed,*" he said. I was just about to open the one he'd handed me when I stopped and quirked my head a bit. "See, it's this thing—you read your fortune and then you add 'in bed' after it." He was smiling, impressed with himself. "Go on," he said.

I shook my head at him. I opened the cookie he'd handed me.

There was no fortune in it.

# 43 • Choice

I had already decided this was our last morning together.

I wasn't going to tell him.

He came down the stairs while I was watching the sun rise over the sound from the window. He walked up behind me, and rested his forehead in the space between my shoulder blades. He wrapped his arms around my waist from behind. He turned his head sideways, nuzzling into me. His hair had grown long enough that it was no longer prickly stubble.

"I know who you are," he said.

I didn't say anything.

"Last night, it was like something clicked in my head. Something...I dunno. Like a puzzle with a piece missing."

I turned around and pulled him into my arms, resting my chin on the top of his head. "Who am I?" I whispered. In that moment, his naked body against my own, I felt connected for the first time. I felt the world.

"Orpheus," he said. Something about hearing that name for the first time from his lips crushed past all the walls I'd built up. He looked up into my eyes. We stood like that for a long time. I think he was waiting for me to try to deny it, but I wasn't going to. "I have so many questions," he said, finally. I didn't say anything, but our eyes never once moved away. "How?" he finally asked.

"The ship won't come for me again," I said. He looked away, and put his cheek against my chest. "So, I wander."

"Did you really go there to try to save her?" he asked.

"Yes," I said.

"And she's really still there?" he asked.

"Yes," I said.

"And me?" he asked. I could tell he was making himself not look up at my face.

"As close as I could ever find."

"Play for me?" he asked, and turned his head so that it was still against me, but he was looking at the stairs. On them was my guitar case. He'd brought it down from the closet.

My instant reaction was to say no, but in that moment, I couldn't. Even knowing it would mean the knock on the door. I couldn't fight it any more. My fingers ached to touch the neck again, to have the cold steel of the strings against them. I walked to the case. Each of the locks squealed as I opened them; they'd been shut so long that I'm sure they'd forgotten that they could move. The guitar was in far worse condition than I had ever imagined. When I put it on my left thigh, though, it fit perfectly, and was already warm.

I looked up at him. "I've been playing it. Sometimes. When you're in the shower or gone to get food. It was the last piece of the puzzle, you see," he said. While he talked, I checked the tuning, and it was still pitch-perfect. For the first time in so long I couldn't even remember, my fingers felt light. Young. "Don't ask me how," he said, "but I could see the marks on the frets where you'd played the same song over and over again." I looked. He was right; the notes of the song I wrote for her wedding day. Back when I had played it, still, back during one of those endless wars. "So, I tried playing those... and a tune just sort of made sense once I heard all the different notes." I played a small repeating melody, then looked at him. He nodded. "I heard it last night in my dream. I think...I think you hummed it. I think you hummed it, and it wound up in my dream, too." He curled his knees up to his chin. "I saw a woman with long brown hair. She was getting ready to be married, but a man came that wasn't...wasn't you," he said. "She ran, and stepped into a nest of snakes," he said. His eyes locked on mine. I nodded. "She was beautiful," he said.

I started to play.

I don't know how long I played, but when I ended the song the sun was streaming in through the window. Jacob was letting tears flow from his eyes and down his cheeks. I put the guitar aside, and he came to curl against me.

"Does that mean that the other part is true, too?" he asked.

"I believe it is."

I could feel him trying to control his fear, "then you're going to have to go, aren't you?"

"Yes."

He tightened his grip on me.

"I don't want you to," he said.

"I don't have a choice."

He leaned back, looked away, and nodded. "How will they find you?"

"The music," I said.

"But—," he said, looking at the guitar.

"It wouldn't matter. If I hummed last night, then they're already on their way," I said, standing, and pulling him up with me. "Which is why you have to go," I said.

"No!" he said.

"Yes. For your own safety, yes—they'd kill you, too."

"But you said you can't die!" he said.

"What they do is different than dying of old age," I said. "Go," I whispered, pointing back up at the bedroom. He looked at me again. To see him resign himself to what was to happen nearly broke my resolve, but I'd seen what they could do. I knew what those things would do to him if he was here when they arrived.

When he came back down dressed and with his duffel, I was already near the door. I knew we didn't have much time to get him safely away. As he got near the door, he whispered, "please." I opened the door. I watched the effort it took for him to make himself go through that door, and the only thing that kept me from giving in was remembering them; their horrible faces. What I'd seen them do to men. He walked like a condemned man to the jeep. I opened the door, and he got in. Before I could close it, he caught it, and whispered "please," again. His eyes locked on mine. I closed the door.

The drive was silent. Only the wind outside the windows made any noise. He was controlling himself, but I could guess at the terrible cost. Still, he would live. As long as he was alive, there would be chances for connection with someone who could give him more than I could. We pulled in to the gate. He signed in with no expression on his face, like a robot. As I pulled the jeep to a stop beside the steps, he turned to me one last time. "Not ever?" he asked.

I shook my head. "They know this place now, if they've tracked me here. I'd be endangering you."

"But...," he began.

"No," I cut him off.

What little bit of life was left in him at that moment drained away. He opened the door, got out, and then closed it. He stood there a moment as if deciding something, then walked up the steps without looking back.

## 44 • Listening

This city is famous for the musicians that come from it. There has always been something about the perspective the continuous rain brings to them. The endless gray sea. I've often thought about going to listen. Some twenty-five year old woman sitting in a bar she hates, playing a guitar that's on its last legs for just enough tip money to buy breakfast in the morning. A kid who gets a toy guitar as a birthday present but goes on to reinvent the way people see music. I've been meaning to go, but like women, I just can't handle dealing with music again.

On the way back to the apartment, I turn the radio on.

The wind is roaring through the window, and I'm listening to music.

# 45 · Flight

I pull the jeep into the parking space. I figure I might just have enough time to get in to the apartment, pack a bag, grab the guitar and then get out of town.

I take the steps two at a time. I have my key out already; I don't want to waste even a second. At least Jacob is safe, though. Whether or not I live through the next hour or so, he's safe. I put the key in the lock.

And the door is already unlocked. It slowly swings open. Through the crack I can see the furniture overturned. I wait for a second, listening with my whole body. I don't hear anything. The guitar is still on the bottom stair where we left it. I've fought men before; this is different. I am afraid for the first time in a very long time.

I walk as quietly as I can in to the apartment. The door sounds like it's shrieking as my shoulder bumps it open a bit. I stop again, listening with every inch of my skin. When I don't hear anything for another few moments, I rush to the guitar. Luckily enough I didn't put it away back upstairs. Though I'm not hearing anything up there, I don't want to take my chances. I put the guitar back into the case. The locks creak closed so loud I'm convinced the neighbors will start shouting at any moment. The snap is like a gunshot.

I turn and walk as quickly as I can out the front door. There were some things I'd like to have packed to take with me, but each second at this point is a tiny little gift from on high. I don't even bother to close or lock the door behind me. I have the guitar, and that's all that matters. I take the steps three at a time, all but hopping down them. I'm sure it looks funny, but nothing about this moment is anything but terrifying.

I make it to the jeep and throw the guitar on to the passenger seat.

I'm just about to climb into the driver's seat when I see something move behind me in the rearview. I freeze. It's one of them.

In the mirror I can see her standing right behind me. She's got on sunglasses, and she looks—normal. Another one comes from behind the building and walks calmly to stand in front of me. She is dressed the exact same way. Dark sunglasses, expensive looking suit. Like an FBI agent.

"Close the door," she says. Jacob told me once that in the movies, when someone has to go back in and re-record their dialogue because a plane was flying overhead, or a strong wind blanked out what they said, they call that additional dialogue recording, or ADR. You can always tell when it happens because the voice suddenly sounds much clearer than it did a second ago, or will in another second. That's because it's done in a booth, in a studio, sometimes months later. The background noises are different; the distance from the microphone is different, so the voice sounds different. Unearthly for a moment. Like it's coming from somewhere outside the moment. That's what her voice sounds like to me.

I see myself closing the door, even though I didn't want to.

She walks right up to me. That's when I see that there are others all around. And I run.

# 46 • A Few Ways

Her boot slams into my mouth, and I fall backward. The back of my head hits the concrete with a hollow sound. For a moment, I'm fascinated by it. Then the pain hits, and I forget sound; I try to get on my side, so that I can get up. Her boot slams into my back. My spine explodes with hurt. She crouches down, and for some reason all I can do is think about how thick the soles of her shoes are. Her hand digs into my hair, and she hauls my head back at an extreme angle from my neck.

"Did you really think you were going to get away?" she asks. This close, she should have a smell, but she doesn't. None of them do. I look around and see the others standing there, looking just like her, watching. Eleven women who look almost exactly like her, even down to the dead expressions under the identical sunglasses.

She shoves my head forward again, and my forehead thunks against the concrete. My skull vibrates without pain, and I think to myself that can't be good. She's still crouched down near my head. I look up right at her crotch. She puts her hand under my chin, and guides my eyes up to her own.

She's taken off the sunglasses.

Her eyes glow pale fire. I'm reminded of the morning not so long ago; the sunrise as I took Jacob back to his school. I wonder where he is, if they've found him, what they've done to him.

As if reading my thoughts, she says "The boy is safe; he bears no part in this. None of them do. This is between you and us."

"The ferryman—," I start to explain when she clenches her fingers, and slams the heel of her hand into the bridge of my nose. All I taste is blood, as something warm drips down my chin.

She smiles, and cups my chin again, bringing my eyes to hers. The fire that glows in them isn't frightening—it is pure, unadulterated otherworld. Her eyes glow with the fury she has been sent here to dispense. For a moment, I wonder if there is ever any way to end such an inexhaustible supply. Then I realize, as her lips crack into a smile, she means to try.

"Were you saying something?" she asks.

Any answer is going to bring just as much retribution as no answer, so I stay silent. Her teeth shine beneath her lips, and I'm reminded of the women on the rocks. I sang to them, and it was just enough of a diversion to save the crew. There will be no such reprieve here, though. Sing, don't sing; these women don't care. It will take my blood to quiet them.

A lot of it.

Her thumb caresses my cheek. "No?" she asks, tilting her face to the side. "Well, then, let's get down to business, shall we?" she asks. She stands, and takes off her jacket. She hands it to one of the other women without saying a word. She turns her back to me and whispers something. The others back away a step, making the circle bigger.

"Stand up," she says, turning around.

I try. I can't move. This is somehow worse than knowing I will die, today. Knowing that someone is seeing me, the warrior that I am, unable to control my body. I try again, with the same result. "Stand," she says, a tone of warning creeping into her voice. I still cannot. She must be able to see me trying. Some small part of me, some part that I have not heard from for a long time, hopes that she can see me trying, and will take pity on me.

I should know better by now.

She bends at the knees, again, crouching. Her hand creeps under my throat, and she grabs my shirt. With one hand, she hauls my entire body to its feet. She continues holding me that way, with one hand, using my gathered collar as a handle. She lowers me to the floor. Her eyes blaze that unearthly fire at me.

"Do you know who we are?" she asks.

I say, "Furies."

She smiles, and I get goosebumps.

"Yes," she says, "We have had quite a time finding you. Albeit, there were other matters to attend to, but nevertheless; you should be quite pleased with yourself. It has taken us a great deal of time and trouble to reach this moment." She turns her side to me, and reaches out for something. One of the other women produces a sword from thin air. A gladius. It gleams like the sun.

She nods to the women behind me. I feel fingers on my shirt, then it is ripped off of me. I hear the button's tiny clatter on the concrete. They echo strangely off the walls in all directions. Her eyes never leave mine.

"How many?" she asks.

"How many what?" I ask in return.

She raises the sword, and draws a fiery line across my chest in one swift motion. My whole body explodes in pain. My rational mind is telling me that there is no way this much pain could come from a sword cut. I have been cut by many blades in my time; none has ever felt like this. What she's holding, then, must be some sort of object; something cooked up by their lame-foot uncle. When my body has cooled enough to allow my mind back into it, I feel the blood dripping down my chest.

I also realize I've gone hoarse from screaming.

Her smile makes me feel tiny, and powerless. For a fleeting second, I wonder if I could fight them. *No,* some ancient thing inside me sighs, *not even gods can fight them when the time comes.*

"How many?" she asks again, coolly observing the sword's edge.

"I don't know what you're—," I start to say.

The swordstroke again. I come back to myself on my knees. My throat is raw and hot.

She's crouched down, so that our faces are at the same level. The sword is point down, like a cane, almost. The reflection shows me twisted, tormented.

"There are a few ways that we can do this, musician. I'm sure even you, failed as you are at the singing of history, must know that. Tell us what we want to know, and this need not be you," she says, motioning toward the blade with her head. The image in the blade writhes in its silent agony. I look back to her eyes.

She means boys. It's very clear, now. Somehow, the boys have something to do with this.

"Boys?" I ask, my throat screaming protest.

Her wicked, jagged smile is all I need to see.

"I never intended—," I start. The blade moves across my cheek so fast I don't even see it. I feel it, though.

I come back to myself lying on my side. She hasn't moved from where she is crouched. My back hurts from the twisting I've been doing. Idly, I wonder how long this has gone on, already.

"At least a hundred," I say, "maybe more."

"Ah, you see?" she says, looking up at her companions. She looks back at me, "Some of my sisters tried to tell me that it was useless to try to talk to you. They said you, being a man, could never be reasonable. *Men are not rational creatures,* they told me. It is a good thing for you I did not listen, eh?"

I move to sit up. My head is swimming from the pain.

"So," she says, cocking her head to the side again, and flicking her hair behind her shoulder with a move of her head. "Why have you tried to subvert the natural order?"

I almost repeat the last part of her question back to her, but stop myself. I don't understand what she means.

Her grin says that she might strike again if I don't answer soon. And she does.

I come back to myself on my side, again, but with a large pool of blood next to my face. The taste of it is all through my mouth. I try to clear as much of it as I can by spitting. I try to sit up. My lungs are scratched raw.

"Why have you tried to subvert the natural order?" she asks, again.

"I never intended to," I blurt before I can stop myself. I brace for another cut.

None comes.

Her eyebrows go up. Even with this comical expression on her face, she still gives off deadly like a perfume. "Really?" she asks. She stands. "Really?" she whispers, again. I can tell she doesn't believe me.

"Do you know what happened the day you prayed for passage across the Styx?" she asks. I shake my head. "We wept," she says, looking directly into my eyes. "We wept. Not many know that. We heard you, and we wept."

"Why?" I ask.

Her eyes fall slowly to the floor, and she smiles wistfully. Even in this soft state, she gives off hatred in waves. She looks back up at me, "because of the power of your love. No one is immune to that; not even us."

"So why this?" I blurt out before I can stop myself.

"Because you are defying that love," she says, leaning in close to me. She cups my chin, and moves in so close I can feel the terrible heat of her skin. "You defy that love and in so doing, you defy the natural order of things. That," she says, "*that* we cannot allow."

# 47 • Wickedness

**N**atural order, human," she says, "ordained systems." She hands the sword to one of the women. She reaches her hand out to another one. That woman produces something golden from thin air. I watch as my torturer slides whatever it is over her fingers, grasping her hand into a fist. They look like tiny shields for her knuckles, and then I understand.

"The way things are meant to be. Men impregnate women, who have children, who go on to be impregnated or to impregnate. It is the way of the universe—order, design. The system is perfect," she says, clenching and unclenching her fist, getting more comfortable with the hunk of gold in her hand.

"You, though," she says, looking directly into my eyes, "You have decided that you are above that, somehow. Not for you to sit on the banks and wait for the riverman to receive his orders for you, is it? No. You decide to commit this—this wickedness—this terrible twisting of the natural order." As she says the word, the wind whistles through the hunk of metal as she swings her fist. I hear the crunch of my jaw echo back to me from the walls.

My head hits the concrete, and I think I hear my brain slosh.

"This is how you choose to keep the memory of your wife, who even now watches from the underworld and weeps," she says.

Next to my mouth, I see a tooth.

"Boys must be left alone. They must grow into men. It was this that brought Greece to its knees, and Rome after it. Boys must not be violated if they are to rule over women. How can they rule their women if they have been made to feel like them? If they have been made soft by taking a lover inside?" she asks, and the wind whistles as she swings again.

"Worse; you make them love you," she says, stepping back.

"They fall in love with you, and then you walk away from them. You not only unman them, you dehumanize them, as well." She kicks my head. It is almost a kindness because it hurts so much less.

"What—," I started, and she kicks me again. I spit blood. I look up at her. She rolls her eyes, and makes a motion with her hand as if to say get on with it. "What are you going to do?" I ask.

She grins, and looks around. Eleven other identical grins. She removes the golden knuckles from her hand. Another of the women takes them. She receives a towel from another woman. She wipes her hands. As she does, she says "I think you know."

And I do. The moment I knew who they were, I knew how this was going to end. The only way it *could* end. She hands the towel back to another of the women. "There is only one punishment possible for such an egregious crime," she says. There is so much of my blood on the ground.

"I didn't ask for this," I say.

"What?" she asks, crouching down again. She leans in closer.

"I didn't ask for this," I say.

"Ah," she says. She looks up at another of the women and nods. That woman leaves the circle. "And what exactly *did* you ask for?" I hear the trunk of a car open. A second later, I hear it close. Footsteps coming back toward the circle.

"I just wanted my wife," I say.

"I see," she says. The woman returns to the circle. My torturer stands, and takes something from her. She crouches down once more. She shows it to me. "Do you know what this is?" she asks.

"No," I say, shaking my head. The world spins for a second.

It is a large white cloth. I can see something wrapped in it. The cloth is flimsy, and tattered. She peels it back one fold at a time, slowly. When she peels away the last fold, I can see a silver ring. I look away from the ring, and to her. She nods. I reach in, my fingers soaking blood into the cloth. I pick up the ring and inside I can see writing. I turn it toward the light, and there are the words I inscribed in the band so long ago.

This is my wife's ring.

As if reading my mind, she says "Her dress, too. Or, at least, what's left of it. Do you understand?"

I look back to her eyes. The fury there has grown hotter. I shake my head no.

She nods, "We didn't think you would. We were told to show you, anyway." She folds the cloth closed once more. She hands it away without looking. For a second, I admire their efficiency; their one-trackness. They came here to do a job; a job they enjoy, but they are in lock step with one another. "The ring is being returned to the mortal world. You see, so long as she kept it, there was some hope. She held on to some hope that you might return," she says.

"But—," I start, "but she was turned into stone—," I stammer.

She laughs, too. "Ah. Yes. And no one has ever been turned back into flesh from stone, have they?" she asks. Her tone tells all. She stands. "Before we carry out the sentence, we've been asked to allow you five minutes," she says. I hear the sound of a car door opening, and then closing.

Footsteps are approaching. As they do, the torturer stands. She moves aside. I try to look up, but the world spins too fast. I look back down at the ground. The footsteps stop, and the circle parts a little. I look up as much as I can. It's very bright; my eyes are swollen and tearing up.

My wife is standing before me.

# 48 • Eurydice

Why is it when you see them again, they steal the breath from your chest? She was stunning. Her hair was perfect, her clothes were perfect, her eyes were hidden behind glasses. It was like armor. I've faced down men in helmets with tall crests that I feared less.

"Hello," she said, her hands going to her hips.

I tried to speak, but couldn't. The Kindly One stepped back some more. My wife and I were alone in the circle they formed at the edge of the light.

"Aren't you going to say anything?" she asked. Her voice was soft, barely controlled fury.

"I don't know what to —," I start.

"No," she interrupted, "of course you don't." She removed her leather gloves and handed them back to one of the circle without looking. Her hands were perfect. "Does he know everything?" she asked over her shoulder.

"No," one of them replied, "we thought it best to leave the explaining to you."

They moved around a bit, the rustling of dead leaves. It took me a few moments to register that as laughter. They were laughing. The lines around her lips showed and she smiled.

She crouched down and removed her glasses in one clean motion. Her eyes hit me so hard, I suck air through my teeth. They glowed the same uncanny green as the rest of the women. She was one of them.

She cocked her head to the side, "See something disturbing, lover?" she asked. Her skin glowed like theirs, only more deadly, somehow. The menace came off her so hard, I had to hold my breath to keep from whimpering. "Do you know why I'm here?" she asked.

I shook my head, happy to have something to concentrate on other than the fear. Her smile flashed again. I tried not to think of a barracuda. "No?" she asked, in a manner one might use with a petulant child. "Am I so easy to forget?" she asked.

"I don't now why you're—," I started.

"Yes," she interrupted, "you've already explained that. It's quite simple, really," she said, and moved closer. I had to stop myself from moving away from her. Something told me that would make this all worse, somehow. She reached out, and brushed my hair away from my face. "Singer of songs, am I so easy to forget?" Her smile went motherly for a moment. She almost seemed warm.

Then her hand came across my face. As strange as it might sound, it hurt worse than anything the blade could have done. When I turned my face back toward her, her teeth showed just behind her lips. That near-smile seemed to say a lot more than she could.

"It's very easy, really: He wanted a wife. I can never be his bride. You were only there for a few moments; you have no idea how hideous and terrible they are," she said, looking down at the concrete. I thought I saw her shiver, then look back at me. "I can never be the bride of a God, and so the only way I can get out of that place, that place you damned me to," she said, and slapped me again, harder somehow, than before. "The only way possible was to become something other than just a wandering shade, listening to the pick-up lines of Achilles for the thirteen-millionth time." With that, in an uncanny gesture of imitation, she stood up, and removed her suit jacket in the exact same manner as my torturer before. She handed it back with the same lack of concern for who took it. She crouched again. She worked the golden knuckles over her own. She grabbed me by my shirt collar and stood me up in one swift motion. I saw her fist go back, and closed my eyes as it pistoned forward. The universe went redblack with pain.

I opened my eyes to find myself on my back, her standing over me. Her fist went back, again, and came forward. The world split with a deafening crack as my skull hit the concrete. "Can you guess what I've decided to become in order to get out of that place? I'll give you three tries." She pulled her fist back again, and then shot it forward. The world cracked again.

I could feel one of my teeth loose on my tongue. I tried to turn my face to the side, so I didn't swallow it, but it was too late. I felt it slide down my throat as her fist came down again.

"That's right; I'm becoming a fury in my own right, lover, song-singer, captain of armies," she said. Her foot went into my ribs. "This is good for me," she said, "but bad for you, I'm afraid." Her foot rammed into the side of my skull. The world rang with a high, far off chime. "In order to do that, I have to do one thing: clear all my connections to the mortal world. Simple enough on paper, but harder in the execution, wouldn't you say?" she said, and her heel came down on my forehead.

"Sister," one of them in the circle said. She stepped away from me. I heard them talking, and I knew something had changed, but I couldn't move my head to see.

"They tell me you've already felt the sword," she said, coming back again. "How did you like it?" she asked, crouching down. I saw her face clearly as she used the sword to balance. The gold of its handle reflected light into her furious green eyes.

"You're going to kill me," I said.

"Yes," she said, "I'm afraid I must. It is the only way for me to become one of them. Eviscerate you," she said, her voice pregnant with anger.

"Jacob—," I said before I could stop myself.

"Oh, don't worry about that. The boy has no reason to fear us. He is but young, and you an immortal," she said, *tsk-tsk*ing through her teeth. She leaned in closer, and I could taste the heat of her breath. "You should have known better."

"Sister," one of the circle said. I recognized the voice as my torturer.

"Yes?" my wife asked.

"He must admit to you that he is who we think before this goes any further," she said. My wife looked up at the ceiling, then exhaled.

"Of course," she said. She looked back down at me, "of course. We knew that, didn't we?" She leaned closer to me, pushing the hair out of my face again. "What is your name?" she asked. I didn't answer, feeling the softness of her hand on my face. She slapped me, and my eyes focused again. "Who are you?" she asked. I stared at her for a moment, seeing in her place some horrible creature, like them.

She put the sword point just above my left eye, "Name?" she asked.

"Orpheus," I said, relishing my name after so long without it. "Orpheus," I said.

"Now, that's better, isn't it?" she asked.

"The River," one of the circle said.

My wife nodded her head without looking back.

# 49 • Animals

The car moved at a steady pace. The vibrations were putting my legs to sleep. I heard a click, and then a deep voice saying "... *for further information. Here at the top of the hour, we return to a story we began reporting last night. It seems that, somehow, several cages at the city Zoo were left open, and a large number of animals escaped. Authorities say that they are working around the clock to attempt to round the animals back up. However, they do say that this could take some time, as it is likely that the animals have all gone different directions. Authorities asked us to caution all listeners; should you see an escaped animal, stay clear. Remember; these animals may have been somewhat domesticated, but they are still animals. Some of them are carnivores, in fact, and may attack humans if they get too close. So, again, be cautious—if you see one of the escaped animals, do not approach it yourself. Get to a phone and alert authorities as soon as possible. And in sports, today..."*

There was another click, and the car went silent again.

Somehow, I knew that was going to be important. I could feel it in my bones. Like seeing a crow on the ground or in a branch, ignoring the people shuffling by it. A bird-sign, an Omen; you're certain that the reason it's not rooting for food on the ground is that it's staring right at you. You wonder if anyone else can see it at all.

# 50 • Silencing Orpheus

Stuffed into the backseat, bound and bleeding, I spent the next thirty minutes listening to my wife breathe. She was alive. She was here, beside me. I hadn't seen her in all of recorded history, and yet here she was beside me. The windows were tinted so dark I couldn't see what was going on outside the car, but I felt the steady downslope of the land. I knew where we were going.

"Did you bring it?" one of the women said to another.

"Yes; it's in the trunk."

My wife smiled at that, but never looked at me.

The car slowly pulled to a stop, and the doors opened. I had to squint, the light cracked through the clouds so vehemently. My wife got out, stood for a moment, then grabbed my arm. She hauled me from the car easily. She was already stronger than she had been back in the parking garage. Her eyes glowed so fiercely, not even the glasses held them back. We started walking. My eyes hadn't adjusted yet, so I could barely see, but I could smell.

The air had gone wet, and salty. I knew where we were.

Behind me, I heard the car door shut. I also heard the trunk open and close. When my eyes adjusted, I could see them all gathered in a circle. My wife and I were standing just outside of it. Beyond was the sea, growing deep ride like wine in the fast fading light.

"Soon," she said to me, "soon." She put her hand on my shoulder. My body tensed in a wave going out from that spot. I slipped into the past for a moment, and remembered the moment I'd seen her.

She had been the quiet one among the giggling girls. I remembered that. She was the one who hid her eyes from me. I think that's what interested me the most. She was the one that I wanted to talk to. I spent the entire feast trying to get close to her, but every time I did, Jason would open his mouth to make a speech, and I had to be attentive. He had his eye on the most brazen of them, Medea. I wasn't interested in *her*. Her eyes held no secrets. I don't think Jason ever looked into them, though. His interest was about three foot south of that.

Even when we were out on the sea, his talk was always of her hips, her breasts. Mine were only of the girl with the eyes that wouldn't let me go. They never did, either. Not even now, with them glowing like the very fires of creation and destruction. She smiled at me, and her hand left my shoulder.

The wind came up, and with her hair flowing behind her, she seemed like a goddess already. I wondered why it was necessary to even involve me in this. She knelt down, and reached into the water. For a split second, I saw her cradle her head against her shoulder, and her eyes close. Her hand came out of the water, and she shook the water from it. Her eyes stayed closed, though, as if she was listening to some other music, just underneath everything I could hear.

"Is it true?" she asked without turning around, "what they say about you and the sirens?"

"Yes," I said.

One of the furies walks past me. She had something covered in a long, black cloth. When she reached my wife, she handed it over. My wife took it, and the other woman stepped back. My wife set the cloth down on the pier. She unwrapped it.

It was my guitar.

She studied it for a moment, and then looked up at me. Her eyes fell back to the guitar. "What song was it you played?"

"Against the women of the rock?" I asked.

She nodded.

"A song I made for you before I even knew you," I said. After a moment, when she said nothing, I added "I knew that, one day, when I was finally home again, I'd find the only woman I'd ever love, and ask her to marry me, and I was going to play it for her, whoever she was, the morning after our wedding."

Her eyes closed, and then opened again. "I see," she said.

She picked up the guitar, cradling it like a child, and walked toward me. She looked to either side of me, and nodded. I felt the bonds holding my hands release. She held the guitar out to me.

"Play," she said.

"I don't understand—," I started to say.

"Play," she said again, and pushed the guitar at me once more.

"Okay," I said, and took the instrument.

I slung the strap over my shoulder, wincing with the pain, as she turned away from me. The wind caught her hair again, and she put her hands in her pockets. I plucked a single string, checking the tuning. I didn't need to, though; this guitar had never gone out of tune. I knew it never would, even when I bought it.

I started to play the song I'd used so long ago. The notes slid off of my fingers. The wind picked up stronger. I lost myself in the playing, and remembered the sea that day. I saw the way the sun played off of the waves, and how beautiful the day would have been if only there had been no danger. I remembered seeing the women on the rock, calling with their terrible voices. They promised me the same things they promised everyone; eternal knowledge. They promised to love us all for the dirty, warring, hateful creatures we were—they knew how seductive that was.

So I'd played the only song I could think of; the one that reminded me most of home. The notes were the ones that made me remember the mystery in her eyes, the ones that recalled the wide pastures and tall rocks. The song I'd written specifically to remind me of her, the woman in my mind who had become the woman standing before me now, intent on killing me when my song was done.

As I played, I noticed that a few birds had landed on the dock. After a moment, there were a few more. Just out to sea, there were some spouts of dolphins coming into the sound. The more I played, the more animals I started to notice, in fact. More birds flitted in. I noticed that the circle of women had to move as more and more animals arrived; stray dogs were walking up to me. Cats had come up from below the pier. I saw a few sand spiders come up the planks. Out in the water, fish were jumping, and the dolphins backs kept moving over the water.

I couldn't stop playing.

I thought maybe I should, but I couldn't.

Then a lion walked through the circle of women as if they

weren't there at all. They moved out of its way. The huge cat walked right up to me, and then lay down on the pier. It looked at me with those fierce yellow eyes, the wind blowing its mane around. Just behind it, an elephant shouldered next to the car. It shook its head a bit, then knelt down. I looked out on the water, and the dolphins had stopped moving; they all had their heads above water, staring at me. Out past them, larger spouts were blowing; whales all coming into the sound. Four more lions had come along, and they were lying next to the huge male, all watching me.

I looked at the women in the circle, and noticed their eyes wrinkled in something like wonder. I looked at my wife, though, and saw only the eternal sad burning in them. I was nearing the end of the song. I think she sensed that.

The blade was out of the scabbard under her jacket and in me before I even saw the gleam. She'd stabbed me through the guitar, plunging the steel deep into my belly. All of the animals let loose a cry, simultaneously. It was strange, but my last thoughts weren't about my pain, but about how beautiful the music of so many voices was. I went to one knee, then the other one dropped.

She pulled the blade from me. I dropped the guitar with a thud. I heard someone scream "NO!" and I turned my head around just in time to see Jacob.

I fell forward, and my cheek slapped against the boards. The women holding Jacob back let him forward. He knelt beside me, crying.

"No," he said, sobbing.

"It's okay," I said, and I knew it would be.

"What am I going to do now?" he asked.

"Whatever you want," I said.

"But—," he stuttered, "but—,"

I reached out, and put my hand against his face. I could see the circle of women taking their jackets off, and pulling knives from sheaths. "Go," I said.

"No," he said.

"Yes," I said, "Go. I'm going to be leaving, soon."

"Go, boy," my wife said to Jacob.

"No," he said. She put her hand on his shoulder, and he shrugged it off.

"Make him go," I said.

She nodded, and then nodded to the women. Two of them took him under the arms and dragged him away. He was sobbing, and reaching for me.

Still standing beside me, my wife asked "The guitar?"

"Whoever needs it," I said. I looked up into her eyes, and they were stone walls. I said "I waited."

Her eyes almost seemed to smile for a second, and then went dead again, "I never asked you to."

"I never loved another," I said.

She shook her head, "Silly man; do you think that simply because you never put yourself into another woman after I was gone that you didn't love? You have loved again and again and again— all of them boys, true, but does that somehow mean you were any less true to your word?" she asked, and laughed one small, joyless laugh. "So like a man; to think that his cock is the important thing," she leaned in close enough that I could smell the smoky savor of her breath, "You said you'd never love another, and yet here I find you, at the end of a string of boys going back centuries. A string of boys that all look like girls with their pants on, and somehow I'm supposed to see this as staying faithful to your vows? Fool."

She picked up the guitar, and I saw the blood soaking into the wood. She tossed it into the sound. It didn't sink; it floated. Bobbing up and down, as if alive, it floated away on the water.

She bent down and stared into my eyes for a long while. "Thank you," I said. She nodded, and even after all she'd said, she put her hand over my eyes. I felt the gentle pressure of that hand, and knew the ceremony was over. The hand I had dreamed of for so long covered my eyelids, and me thinking 'her fingers are so warm'.

The rest was blackness.

# Epilogue: Down the River

Even before she picks up the paper, she's thinking 'gotta' write a song, today.' The band will be at the studio in less than an hour. She told them she had eleven songs to lay down when she only had ten. She figured the last one would come, but as usual, it didn't.

From the bedroom, last night's...whatever...starts to wake up. She opens the paper, then looks past it at him. He's not as good looking as he was in the dark. 'I have got to stop drinking so much,' she thinks. Still, he's not too bad. She goes back to the paper and tries not to think about the cursor blinking on the laptop sitting just behind it. Each little wink in and out like a little "fuck you" from the Goddess.

Local Musician Dismembered she reads.

A local thirty-something man's body was found gruesomely dismembered
    early this morning. No identification could be found on the John Doe; the
    only evidence was an old guitar found floating nearby with blood soaked into
    the wood.

She stopped reading, tossed the paper aside, and her hands flew to the keyboard of the laptop.

A decade later, when she tells the story to the interviewer who asks "And what about the song 'I'll Keep Your Guitar' from your second album; what inspired that one?" "Well," she says as the camera zooms in for a closeup, "that one was strange; I remember that I didn't have long to get a song written and get to the studio.

I was late as usual." They both smile. "Then I read this story about a man who was murdered and no one could identify him. The only thing they found nearby was an old beat to fuck and back acoustic guitar. Floating in the sound, mind you. So cheap it didn't even sink. Blood all over it. And I got to thinking, isn't that all of us? Musicians, I mean. Isn't that how we live our lives? In the end, we'll all be killed and dismembered, and all that'll be left is our bloody guitars floating away on the current." She waits for a moment. Then says, "of course, the second the song came out there were a whole bunch of imitators."

"That album was the one that launched your eventual success, wasn't it?"

"Yeah; Platinum. And this in the days of illegal downloading, too, so that was quite something."

"If you're just joining us, we're talking with recording artist Sappho on the show tonight. We'll be back in a moment." The camera backs away a bit, and she looks off into space as if listening to someone else. The segment goes black for commercial.